PRAISE

"The Gears are the preeminent historical novelists of our times, offering fascinating and brilliantly researched insights into war, suffering, tribal life, and the beliefs that inspire people to act above and beyond what they thought possible. No one reads a Gear novel without being transformed in beautiful ways. The Gears, separately and together, rank among the most significant novelists of modern times, and their work will endure for generations."

— RICHARD S. WHEELER

"The multitalented Gears, husband-and-wife archaeologists and bestselling authors, score a literary bull's-eye as they weave another vivid narrative thread into their stunning tapestry of Native Americans... The Gears continue to do a magnificent job of advancing a fascinating historical chronicle via action, adventure, and archeology."

— *BOOKLIST*

"Rich in cultural detail. Both longtime fans and newcomers will be satisfied. Another fine entry in an ambitious, long-running series."

— *KIRKUS REVIEWS*

PEOPLE OF THE LONGHOUSE

ALSO BY W. MICHAEL GEAR AND KATHLEEN O'NEAL GEAR

Big Horn Legacy

Dark Inheritance

The Foundation

Fracture Event

Long Ride Home

The Mourning War

Raising Abel

Rebel Hearts Anthology

Sand in the Wind

Thin Moon and Cold Mist

Black Falcon Nation Series

Flight of the Hawk Series

The Moundville Duology

Saga of a Mountain Sage Series

The Wyoming Chronicles

The Anasazi Mysteries

PEOPLE OF THE LONGHOUSE

THE PEACEMAKER'S TALE
BOOK ONE

W. MICHAEL GEAR

KATHLEEN O'NEAL GEAR

People of the Longhouse
Paperback Edition
Copyright © 2024 (As Revised) W. Michael Gear and Kathleen O'Neal Gear

Wolfpack Publishing
701 S. Howard Ave. 106-324
Tampa, Florida 33609

wolfpackpublishing.com

All rights reserved. No part of this book may be reproduced by any means without the prior written consent of the publisher, other than brief quotes for reviews.

This book is a work of fiction. Any references to historical events, real people or real places are used fictitiously. Other names, characters, places and events are products of the author's imagination, and any resemblance to actual events, places or persons, living or dead, is entirely coincidental.

Illustrations by Ellisa Mitchel.

Paperback ISBN 978-1-63977-169-1
eBook ISBN 978-1-63977-168-4

To Tim, Maria, Brandon, and Connor O'Neal, for the sacrifices you made while caring for our mother in her last difficult years. No one could have been kinder, or taken better care of her. We know it wasn't easy. You'll always have a special place in our hearts.

ACKNOWLEDGMENTS

We could not have written the *Peacemaker Saga* series without the dedication and hard work of our archaeological colleagues, many of whom have spent their lives trying to understand the prehistory of this continent. In writing this book, we relied heavily upon the work of Bruce Trigger, Dean Snow, James Tuck, Elisabeth Tooker, William Ritchie, Christina Rieth, John Hart, Mary Ann Levine, Kenneth Sassaman, Michael Nassaney, and Paul Wallace. We are especially grateful to Dr. David Dye, University of Memphis, for his work on prehistoric war and peace movements in the eastern United States.

In addition, the detailed analysis by Barbara Mann and Jerry Fields with regard to dating the founding of the League was very informative. Their article can be found at www.wampumchronicles.com/signinthesky.html; it contains a thorough discussion of the historical record and Iroquoian oral history, and provides an excellent cultural context for dating the famed eclipse.

Lastly, we would like to offer our sincere

thanks to Catherine Crumpler, and the Hot Springs County Counseling Center in Thermopolis, Wyoming, for their help in understanding the psychological responses of children undergoing extreme stress. Those lengthy discussions were not wasted, Catherine. Thanks for sharing your expertise.

NON-FICTION INTRODUCTION

There are eight parts in the Peacemaker Saga. The first four parts, *People of the Longhouse, Shadowed Forest, The Dawn Country,* and *The Bitter Tears* will focus on the early lives of two of the most important, and least known, heroes in world history: Dekanawida and Hiyawento.

The last four parts of the Peacemaker Saga will chronicle their later lives, along with telling the story of Jigonsaseh, who can justifiably be called "The Mother of American Democracy."

Without these three people and their struggle for peace in fifteenth-century North America, it's doubtful that any of the ideals we cherish as free people would exist today.

In fact, it's doubtful that The Free World would exist today.

Let's talk about the origins of Northern

Iroquoians; it's is a hotly debated and very complex topic among archaeologists, but generally we agree that the period from roughly AD 1000-1300 demonstrates fluid and shifting alliances, expanding trade networks, and changing settlement patterns. One thing is for certain: Early Iroquoian cultures were remarkably adaptable and diverse.

Most archaeologists divide Iroquoian culture into three periods: The Early Iroquoian period from AD 1000-1300, the Middle Iroquoian period from AD 1300-1350, and Late Iroquoian from AD 1350 to European contact. For the purposes of this introduction, the Early Iroquoian period is particularly important. Not because it was the apogee of the culture—it wasn't—but because something dramatic happened. At around AD 1000, most Iroquoian peoples lived in small fishing villages or farming hamlets, primarily along rivers where they had good fertile soils and easy access to water. Toward the end of this period, they began moving away from watercourses and started building their villages atop easily defensible hilltops. Some were palisaded—for example, the Bates site in Chenango County and the Sackett site near Canandaigua, New York, both of which date to the thirteenth century.

It is also likely that during the Early period, Iroquoian societies changed from being patrilineal and patrilocal—meaning they traced descent through the male, and women came to live with their husband's family—to being matrilineal and matrilocal, in which they traced descent through the female and after marriage a man moved in with his wife's family.

During the thirteenth and fourteenth centuries, the size of Iroquois villages began to grow. Archaeologists call this "population aggregation," meaning that more and more people were crowding together within the palisaded walls of villages. We see these expanded longhouses at places like the Furnace Brook and Howlett Hill sites in New York, where archaeologists excavated houses that were 210 and 334 feet long. This Middle Iroquoian period also saw the people becoming increasingly dependent upon maize-bean-squash agriculture. As in historic times, men probably cleared the fields, built the houses, and hunted, while women were the farmers. They cultivated the soil, planted, tended the fields, harvested and stored the crops. When women began to account for more and more of the food, their lineages also probably became the dominant social avenue for prestige.

At around AD 1400, the first evidence for individual tribes appears. Differences in pottery styles, burial customs, and types of houses demonstrate divisions between Iroquoian groups. As well, small villages begin to amalgamate with larger ones, forming cohesive social groups, or, we suspect, nations.

AD 1400 is also the time when the Iroquois were building the most impressive longhouses, and many were elaborately fortified. At the Schoff site outside Onondaga, New York, the people constructed a longhouse 400 feet long, 22 feet wide, and nearly as tall. The palisaded settlement may have housed 1,500 to 2,000 people, consisting of many different clans.

As those of you who've read our previous books know, often this type of aggregation is a telltale sign for archaeologists of interpersonal violence. Simply put, people crowd together for defensive purposes. This is also when cannibalism first appears in the Iroquoian archaeological record in the form of cut and cooked human bones.

People of the Longhouse takes place at this critical moment in time.

Why did warfare break out? The fact that the climate had grown cooler and drier certainly contributed to the violence. We know that droughts were more frequent, growing seasons shorter, and food shortages probably more common. As well, larger villages deplete resources at a faster rate. Game populations, nut forests, firewood, and fertile soils would all have played out more quickly, which means they must have had to move their villages more often. Moving may have brought them into conflict with neighbors who needed the resources just as desperately.

The warfare, we know, was violent.

At the Alhart site in the Oak Orchard Creek drainage in western New York, archaeologists found evidence of burned longhouses and food, and the dismembered remains of seventeen people —most of them male. Historically, it was common practice for women and children to either be killed on site, or taken captive and marched away while the male warriors were tortured and killed. At this site, the fragments of a child's skull were found in one storage pit, and the skull of a woman in another storage pit. As well, fifteen male skulls were found in a storage pit on top of charred corn, and were probably placed there as severed heads, in the flesh. Some of them were burned. Two had suffered blows to the front of the head.

At the Draper site northeast of Toronto, fourteen burials date to this period. One burial, an old man, was missing both arms and his shoulder blades. A chert arrow point was embedded in his right hip bone—the femoral neck. There was also evidence that he had been speared in the chest, and scalped. As well, he had sustained a severe blow to the left side of his head, and showed cut marks from having been dismembered. Dismembering the enemy was historically a method of stopping the soul from taking revenge upon its killers; dismemberment apparently immobilized the angry spirit of the dead.

The Van Oordt site, a late fourteenth to early fifteenth-century site near Kitchener, Ontario, revealed thirteen burials. One had fragments of three arrow points embedded in his bones. He also showed signs of numerous puncture wounds; which means he was stabbed several times. Then, both of his arms were severed, and he was beheaded.

At the Cameron site near Lima, New York, a young male burial was discovered. He'd been burned, and showed signs of having been stabbed and scalped. Afterward, his skull was broken open, probably to extract the brain. The interesting thing here is that this young man was buried in the village cemetery, not in a refuse midden. This may mean that his body was found by his relatives and brought home for proper burial.

As well, artifacts made from human bone are plentiful on Northern Iroquoian sites that date from the late fourteenth through the early sixteenth centuries. For example, two skulls were found at the Parsons site in Toronto. The Parsons site was an elaborately palisaded fifteenth-century village. The two skulls, one male and one female, were found in a trash pit inside the inner palisade. Many other human bone artifacts are found in similar "refuse" situations. Human skull pendants or rattles are found across Ontario and New York at the Moatfield, Winking Bull, Uren, Pound, Crawford Lake, Jarrett-Lahmer, Draper, Keffer, Lawson, Campbell, Clearview, Parsons, Bee-ton, Roebuck, Lite, Salem, and Glenbrook sites. Often, the skulls, or skull fragments, have cut marks made by stone tools that are suggestive of scalping. As you already know from earlier paragraphs, scalping was not a French custom brought to the New World and adopted by the tribes; it existed long before Europeans arrived. Such skulls were found at the Draper, Keffer, and Lawson sites. Ground and polished fibulas and femurs—leg bones—as well as arm bones—radii—were used for beads and scraping tools. Pierced mandibles—jaws—and finger and toe bones were used as pendants. Ulnae —arm bones—became awls or daggers, and were also strung as beads. Why is it important to archaeologists that all these artifacts were found in trash middens? Because Iroquoian peoples took very good care of their dead relatives. They had lengthy and beautiful burial rituals to make certain their loved ones reached the Land of the Dead. Since these human remains were not properly cared for, it suggests the bones may have come from less valuable members of society, like enemy captives.

Let's take a few moments to discuss the Iroquoian perspective on captives. By the 1400s, as it was in historic times, warfare and raiding for captives was probably the most important method of gaining prestige in Northern Iroquoian societies. When a person died, the spiritual power of the clan was diminished, especially if that person had been a community leader. The places of missing family members literally remained vacant until they could be "replaced," and their spiritual power—which was embodied in their name—transferred to another person.

Historical records tell us that during the 1600s, the Iroquois dispatched war parties whose sole intent was to bring home captives to replace family members and restore the spiritual strength of the clans. These were called "mourning wars." Clan matrons usually organized the war parties and ordered their warriors to bring them captives suitable for adoption to assuage their grief and restock the village. Once the clan had a suitable replacement, the captive underwent the Requickening Ceremony. In this ritual, the dead person's soul was "raised up" and transferred to the captive, along with his or her name.

This may seem odd to modern readers, but keep the religious context in mind. The Iroquois believed that the souls of those who died violently could not find the Path of Souls in the sky that led to the Land of the Dead. They were excluded from the afterlife and doomed to spend eternity wandering the earth, seeking revenge. However, such souls could find rest if they were transferred—along with their name—to the body of another person. In a very concrete way, the relatives of the dead person were trying to save him.

The souls of men and women killed in battles that were not "raised up" were believed, according to some Seneca traditions, to move into trees. It was these trees with indwelling warrior spirits that the People cut to serve as palisade logs, thereby surrounding the village with Standing Warriors.

Who was fighting? We're fairly sure the warfare was between neighbors, not marauding armies seeking out distant enemies. Why? Archaeologists do craniometric analyses—measurements of skulls—and compare them with other populations to determine their differences or similarities, which indicate probable genetic relationships. In 1998, Dupras and Pratte conducted a detailed study of skulls from the Parsons site and compared them with four other groups, two local—from the nearby Kleinberg and Uxbridge sites—and two more distant groups—Roebuck and Broughton Hill sites in New York. The similarities in the skulls suggest that they came from local populations and probably represented "trophy" heads. Which means they weren't fighting invading strangers—they knew each other.

Iroquoian oral history speaks of this as a particularly brutal time, and clearly the archaeological record supports their stories.

But the violence was also the catalyst for one of the most important events in the history of the world. It led to the rise of a legendary hero, the Peacemaker named Dekanawida, who established the Great Law of Peace and founded the League of the Iroquois—a confederacy of five tribes: the Onondaga, Oneida, Mohawk, Cayuga, and Seneca.

Without the League, the United States would not exist today, nor would our unique understanding of democracy. Concepts like one-person/one-vote or referendum and recall were not European. They were Iroquoian.

And they would prove to be irresistible to the wave of colonists fleeing oppression in Europe.

In 1775, James Adair wrote a book called *History of the American Indian,* in which he described the Iroquoian system of government by saying, "Their whole constitution breathes nothing but liberty...[T]here is equality of condition, manners, and privileges..."

Indeed, the system of government espoused by the League was everything that European monarchies were not. The Iroquois refused to put power in the hands of any single person, lest that power be abused. The League sought to maximize individual freedoms and minimize governmental interference in people's lives. The League taught that a system of government should preserve individual rights while striving to ensure the public welfare; it should reward initiative, champion tolerance, and establish inalienable human rights. They accepted as fact that men and women were equal and respected the diversity of peoples, their religions, economic and political ideals, and their dreams.

Thomas Jefferson wrote, "There is an error into which most of the speculators on government have fallen, and which the well-known state of society of our Indians ought, before now, to have corrected. In their hypothesis of the origin of government, they suppose it to have commenced in the patriarchial or monarchial form...Indian leaders influence them by their character alone...every man, with them, is perfectly free to follow his own inclinations. But if, in doing this, he violates the rights of another...he is punished by the disesteem of society, or...if serious, he is tomahawked as a serious enemy."

On the eve of the American Revolution in 1776, English papers began circulating the following account, which was, incidentally, meant to be insulting: "The darling passion of the American is liberty, and that in its fullest extent; nor is it the original natives only to whom this passion is confined; our colonists sent thither seem to have imbibed the same principles."

Indeed, they had.

Gifted writers like Thomas Jefferson and Benjamin Franklin would openly fan the flames of that "passion" for liberty, and set in motion a chain reaction that has yet to end. That passion would become a sweeping wildfire that would race around the globe and shape the very heart of what would, centuries later, become known as The Free World.

Dekanawida, quite simply, changed the course of history.

We can only imagine the terrifying forces that might have hardened his resolve...

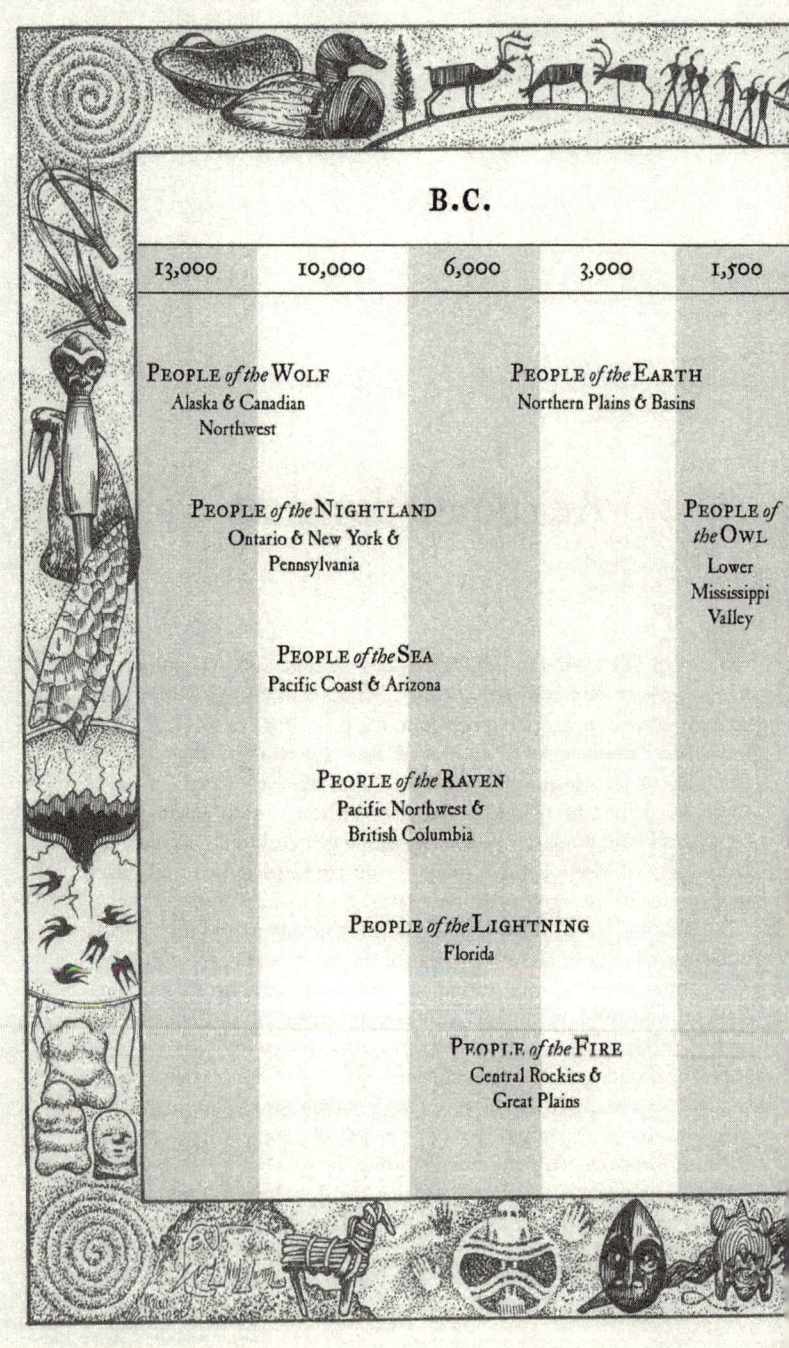

B.C.

| 13,000 | 10,000 | 6,000 | 3,000 | 1,500 |

PEOPLE *of the* WOLF
Alaska & Canadian Northwest

PEOPLE *of the* EARTH
Northern Plains & Basins

PEOPLE *of the* NIGHTLAND
Ontario & New York & Pennsylvania

PEOPLE *of* the OWL
Lower Mississippi Valley

PEOPLE *of the* SEA
Pacific Coast & Arizona

PEOPLE *of the* RAVEN
Pacific Northwest & British Columbia

PEOPLE *of the* LIGHTNING
Florida

PEOPLE *of the* FIRE
Central Rockies & Great Plains

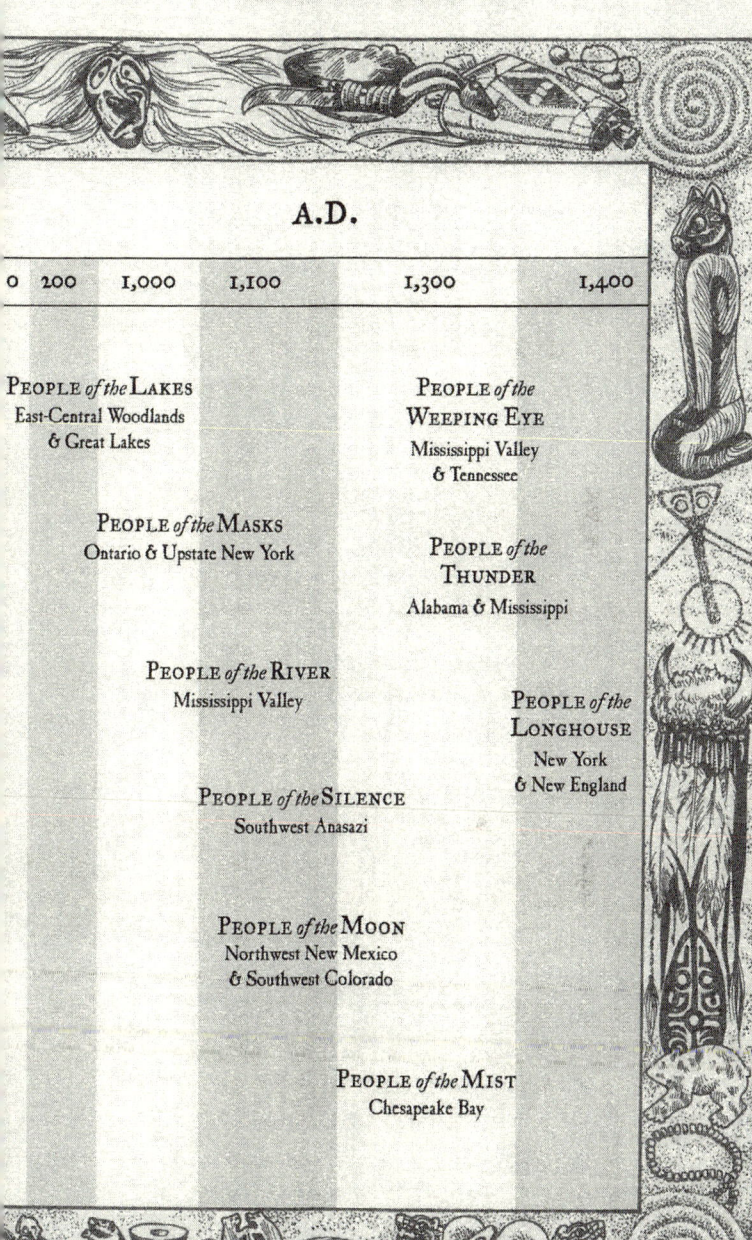

A.D.

| 200 | 1,000 | 1,100 | 1,300 | 1,400 |

PEOPLE *of the* **LAKES**
East-Central Woodlands
& Great Lakes

PEOPLE *of the* **WEEPING EYE**
Mississippi Valley
& Tennessee

PEOPLE *of the* **MASKS**
Ontario & Upstate New York

PEOPLE *of the* **THUNDER**
Alabama & Mississippi

PEOPLE *of the* **RIVER**
Mississippi Valley

PEOPLE *of the* **LONGHOUSE**
New York
& New England

PEOPLE *of the* **SILENCE**
Southwest Anasazi

PEOPLE *of the* **MOON**
Northwest New Mexico
& Southwest Colorado

PEOPLE *of the* **MIST**
Chesapeake Bay

PEOPLE OF THE LONGHOUSE

1

The call still echoed from the depths of the trees.

It made Sky Messenger push onward, down the leaf-strewn trail and into the dark filigree of shadows where glinting eyes watched him from the branches. Night was falling. Soon the owls would lift into the air and vanish like smoke on a windy day, but for now, their gazes fixed on the strange old man with the limp.

He cocked his head, listening. The call was growing fainter. Sky Messenger propped his walking stick and continued on down the trail.

He'd first heard the Voice when he'd seen eleven summers. Since that time, the great unrest came upon him every Moon of Falling Leaves. He would be sleeping warmly beneath his hides, his soul walking through springtime meadows with his Ancestors, when suddenly his eyes would jerk open, and he would sit up in bed. It always began as a low keening. When he heard it, he would jump to his feet and dash out into the cold darkness. On and on he would run, as fast as his bad legs would carry him, away from the village and down the forest trails where bears and wolves prowled.

Four nights ago, he'd leaped from his hides, breathing as though slapped awake, and known the caller was close. The hair at the nape of his neck had stood on end. From far out in the trees, the Voice came, clear and crisp, more real than ever before—*Odion...Odion.* He'd thrown on his cape, for his old body needed it these days, and rushed outside into the icy woods. It was unlike any human voice he'd ever heard, composed of many notes, like an eerie song. And he knew it, knew the speaker, in the depths of his heart, as he had never known another human being.

Sometimes he pursued the Voice all moon long, looking for it as though it were real. Speaking gently or shouting in desperation, he would limp along the trails like a madman. He used his crooked walking stick to probe beneath fallen logs, or stab into holes in the forest floor where supernatural creatures lived; or he would crouch in the underbrush for days, his eyes wide, sniffing the wind for that otherworldly scent he knew would someday be there. Listening. Always listening for that mysterious voice that called him by name, filling him with wild desires and a vague, sweet gladness.

His obsession frightened his children and grandchildren. His clan had begun to say that he was insane, that he was chasing his own afterlife soul that had wandered away into the forest and become lost. None of that mattered. He *knew* he had to find the caller and look him in the eyes.

Sky Messenger stopped to take a breath and looked up into the overarching branches of a hickory tree. He especially enjoyed these rare autumn evenings when he could stand beneath the trees and hear them snapping and cracking as the night cooled.

The Voice faded.

Sky Messenger propped his walking stick and held his breath, listening. In the moonlight, the snow-coated trees had a bluish gleam that seemed to radiate outward into the air, turning it liquid and faintly silver. Deep autumn leaves rustled around his moccasins as he cupped a hand to his mouth and called, "Where are you?"

He searched the forest until he spied movement among the shadows. Concentrating, he thought he saw a black silhouette, standing tall and straight, its arms open to the night sky. Heat flushed his face. Was it real? Was it a...a man? Or did it have wings? Black wings that sleeked down its back? Or perhaps the hump was just a bulky Trader's pack?

He slowly moved toward it. He was afraid of falling. His old bones had grown brittle, and he knew that a simple broken arm might kill him. As he sneaked closer, the Voice lowered its arms and turned toward him.

Odion. Are you coming?

For the first time since he'd seen eleven summers, he was looking into the dark holes of its eyes. Terror made his hands tremble.

"Th-that was my childhood name. They call me Sky Messenger now."

Hunched over, he limped toward the Forest Spirit, his ancient body aching. Every step was at once a threat and a gesture of love and need. The Voice seemed to sense it. Like all predators, they feared each other. It cocked its head, and its eyes caught the starlight and shimmered as though dusted with quartz crystals.

A fleeting instant later, it dashed out into the trees with twigs cracking in its wake.

"No, wait! Come back!"

Sky Messenger stumbled after it, thrashing wildly through the brush, trying to catch up. He chased it straight into a meadow where the starlight reflected so brilliantly from the snow that the

Voice's dark silhouette seemed to be floating above the ground.

"What do you want? Why do you keep calling me? You've been calling me for sixty-five summers."

The creature growled like a cornered wolf, its arms extended as though preparing to take flight.

In a motion as old as predators themselves, Sky Messenger took a step backward, yielding the moment to his opponent, and slowly began to circle around the tree-lined edge of the meadow. He poked at rocks with his walking stick, and sniffed damp tree bark, precisely like the demented old man people claimed him to be. The Spirit kept cocking its head, watching curiously, and after a time, it quieted and lowered its arms. But its quartz-dust eyes remained focused on Sky Messenger, charting his methodical progress around the meadow.

It stunned him that the Spirit seemed suspicious and afraid. What could an old man do to harm a Spirit? Then again, maybe it wasn't harm the Spirit feared. Perhaps it was just the way of the chase. Run and feint. Let your prey catch up, then whirl around and snap at it, and keep it at bay until the final moment. The final lunge for the throat.

Sky Messenger saw his chance and dashed out into the meadow, heading directly for the Voice... and the chase resumed.

Time and again he cornered the creature and tried to force it to answer his questions before it darted away. He stumbled after it in some incomprehensible ancient dance. Was it just a man? Sometimes he thought so. But why would a strong young man let Sky Messenger catch him? The Voice ran until Sky Messenger was right on its heels; then it whirled around snarling. He would never have caught the Voice if it did not wish to be caught. Surely this was some Spirit game.

He halted, breathing hard, and let his gaze drift over the brush and trees.

I'm here, Odion.

He saw it. The Voice stood just ahead, hidden behind a frost-covered dogwood. Its eyes gleamed through the dark weave of branches.

Come...Follow me.

It trotted away, repeatedly looking back over its shoulder, as if to make certain he was still behind; then it disappeared into the forest.

Sky Messenger worked his way down a winding forest trail dappled with snow and frost-rimmed leaves, simultaneously fearing and eager for what he would next see.

"Where are you?" he called. "I've lost you."

From the dark depths of the forest came the call—a long, drawn-out wail, his name in the voice of a wolf, howled with chilling effect.

Sky Messenger's bony fingers tightened around

the knob of his walking stick. He was close now. Very close, and he dared not be afraid of what would come. He swallowed hard and limped forward.

On the other side of a birch copse, the trail sloped upward to a high point overlooking a hilly country filled with great stretches of forests and shining creeks.

Odion.

There. On the trail below.

The Voice let him get to within thirty paces, and started slowly walking away.

Through endless towering trees, Sky Messenger followed, step after step, always twenty paces behind, until Elder Brother Sun rose red over the eastern horizon. As the air warmed, an exotic flowery fragrance wafted around him. His nostrils quivered. He took a deep breath, filling his lungs with the otherworldly sweetness, and his old heart began to slam against his ribs. *That scent!*

In the distance, he saw flocks of birds gathered over a bridge, fluttering, waiting. All along the planks of the bridge, mice darted, their furred backs shining in the newborn light. There were other animals, too. A white-tailed doe, and a lean young wolf.

At the sight of the wolf, tears traced warm lines down Sky Messenger's wrinkled cheeks. He had been running from this moment his entire life. He whispered, "Hello, old friend."

The Voice stopped dead in the trail and let him advance to stand at its side. Sky Messenger shivered. He understood now.

He was answering the last call, walking at the side of the only brother who truly mattered. The brother who had always been there, as unobtrusive as his own shadow, watching over him, fighting at his side on the darkest days.

"You can tell me now," he said, and took a breath to prepare himself. "What is your name?"

The Voice hissed, the sound like a truce being broken by an arrow, and he thought he made out the word *Sonon*.

"Sonon?"

Yes, do you remember me, Odion?

Ancient memories flooded up from behind doors buried deep in his heart, doors Sky Messenger had kept barricaded for sixty-five summers. Behind them, monsters still lived and breathed.

He shook his head and stumbled backward. "No. No, I—I can't—!"

Remember, Odion. You must remember now. It's time.

All of the doors he had so carefully guarded vanished, and a sea of ghostly eyes started coming toward him.

Shuddering, Sky Messenger sank down in the trail and squeezed his eyes closed. As the monsters surrounded him, terror swept him back in time to that long-ago day when this journey had truly started...

2
ODION

The patter of rain falling through branches fills the forest and mixes eerily with the laughter of warriors. The sound of children's feet wading through deep autumn leaves is loud.

I dare to glance up. The storm has sucked the color from the trees. The giant oak trunks look black, their branches iron-gray. We are not on a trail, but march through scrubby underbrush. Ahead of me, one boy and four girls walk with their heads down. Some weep softly, but mostly they are as silent as the dead relatives they left behind in their burned villages.

As the enemy warriors herd us up a steep mountain trail, I see a small clearing ahead. Patches of sunlight penetrate the dark clouds and briefly blaze through the brilliant maples and hickory trees. They seem almost too bright. Painful. I squint and force my legs to keep walking until the clouds swallow Elder Brother Sun again.

I am young, eleven summers, and not yet a man. For as long as I can recall, I have feared that this day would come. Warfare rages throughout our country. Many villages have been attacked, and women and children taken as slaves. Now that I am one of them, I feel like a duck hit in the head with a rock—too numb to think.

When we enter the clearing, four white-tailed deer bound away, and I watch them with my heart racing. They are free…as I was yesterday.

The girl in line ahead of me stumbles. The warriors curse her as she regains her balance. Her name is Agres. She wears a beautiful white doe-hide dress. She arrived last night, and carries an infant in her arms. We all assume the baby is her sister.

I stare at the holes in the soles of the infant's moccasins. My People, the People of the Standing Stone, have a saying: *An infant's life is as the thinness of a maple leaf.* We believe that each person has two souls: a soul that stays with the body forever, and an afterlife soul that travels to the Land of the Dead. Babies are just barely separated from the Spirit world, and vulnerable to being stolen back by unseen ghosts who follow their mothers. The holes tell the ghosts to stay back, and that this child's souls have been claimed by the living.

"Agres should throw away those moccasins," I

whisper. If ghosts take the baby's souls, she will be reborn in a new body and won't have to face what lies ahead for the rest of us.

My eight-summers-old sister, Tutelo, tightens her grip on my hand and looks up. "What, Odion? What did you say?"

Tutelo has a pretty oval face with bright brown eyes. A long black braid hangs down the back of her tan dress. Tiny circlets of copper decorate her sleeves and hem.

"Nothing," I answer, and squeeze her small hand. "Don't talk, Tutelo. You know it causes troub—"

One of the Mountain People warriors—the one I have named Broken Teeth because of the jagged yellow teeth that fill his mouth—glares at me. I quickly look away.

Four warriors guard us. Each carries a bow and has a quiver filled with arrows slung over his left shoulder. War clubs and stone knives hang from their belts. Big Man, the one in charge, really scares me. He has a heavily scarred face, and every time he looks back at the line of children, his jaw clenches with hate. Tutelo whispers, "Where's Mother?"

"Shh."

Tutelo has been asking the same question since midnight. Our mother is War Chief Koracoo. Yesterday morning, Mother led half of our warriors into the forests to scout for the enemy. Father, her deputy, was in charge of defending our village. The attack came at dusk; it was swift and brutal. The People of the Mountain brought three times as many warriors to the fight. Yellowtail Village didn't have a chance.

I remember little of it... Father dragging us out of our beds and ordering us to run...longhouses burning...screaming people racing through the firelit darkness...dead bodies. Then standing in the forest, clutching Tutelo's hand, stunned, as enemy warriors rounded us up and marched us away as slaves. I must have more memories—somewhere inside me—but I cannot find them.

I don't know if Mother and Father are alive, but I keep praying they are. If they survived, they are tracking us, coming for us.

Big Man holds up a hand. We all stop, and out in the forest I hear people moving. I search the shadows and see them weaving among the smoke-colored trunks. One warrior emerges, shoving three girls in front of him. All are beautiful, and have seen perhaps twelve or thirteen summers. The new warrior forces them to join our group.

No one speaks. We just stare at each other in fear and disbelief. The same thing happened last night. That's when Agres and her sister arrived. Big Man has made four stops so far. The red quill patterns on the new girls' capes mark them as Flint People. Was their village also attacked?

Mother says the warfare must stop. She hates it.

Father calls her a "peacemaker," and it always sounds like an insult.

Big Man studies the girls carefully, walking around them several times before he nods and hands over a heavy hide sack to the man who brought the girls. The man shakes it, smiles, and disappears into the trees like mist vanishing on a warm day.

They did not say a word. Have they made this kind of exchange so often they do not need to speak?

Big Man lifts his hand again, and we march, heading east through the sun-dappled forest.

"Where's Mother?"

"Stop asking, Tutelo!"

Tears fill my sister's eyes, but she knows better than to cry out loud. We have each taken a beating for crying. Instead, Tutelo clutches my hand in a death grip and sobs without a sound. My souls shrivel.

I lean down to whisper, "She's coming, Tutelo, but we have to stop talking about it, or the bad men will hear us. You don't want them to know Mother's coming, do you? If they know she's coming, they will ambush her. We must be quiet."

Tutelo looks up with big, tear-filled eyes. In sudden understanding, she whispers, "All right."

As we march deeper into the trees, the scents of rotting wood and damp autumn leaves fill the air. I take a deep breath and let it out slowly.

I keep praying that Big Man told us the truth: We will all be adopted into new families. We will have lots to eat, and though the work will be hard, our new families will come to love us. In time, Big Man says, we will forget our Standing Stone families and be happy in the Mountain People's villages. I will become a great hunter, and Tutelo will marry a good man and give the nation healthy sons and daughters.

Usually, that's how it works. I have seen many children, taken in warfare, brought to Yellowtail Village and adopted into families. Each is miserable at first, but within a few summers, he or she seems genuinely happy. I myself was captured in a war raid. Father says I had seen six or seven moons. He pulled me from the burning wreckage of a longhouse and carried me home to Yellowtail Village. I know no other home, and I love my adopted parents with all my heart. Mother says that no people can create an empire; they must *become* one, and the best way to do that is to adopt conquered peoples into Standing Stone families and educate them as their own children, without distinction.

Unfortunately, I am beginning to think that Big Man's promises of happiness are worthless.

These are not ordinary warriors. Even I can see that. They wear no clan sashes, and have no visible tattoos. In fact, I can spot places where they have cut off tattoos, or obliterated them. They never call each other by name, which makes me think they are afraid that one of us will later speak that name in the wrong company.

Broken Teeth trots toward Agres and her sister. All morning long his eyes have sought out Agres, and I do not like the way he looks at her. Agres wears beautiful polished copper earspools, and shell bracelets that click when she walks. She turns away and tries not to notice Broken Teeth's attention. Instead, she occupies herself with caring for her infant sister. The hungry baby mews constantly. Though Agres keeps placing a wet twist of hide in the infant's mouth to suck on, the baby just spits it out, wails, and tugs at Agres' long hair with frantic hands. None of us has had anything to eat, and water only eases the cramps for so long.

As we walk, the endless mountains pass by. In the afternoon, we enter a stand of enormous oaks. Big Man forces us to climb over bare, exposed rock. Stones are the bones of Great Grandmother Earth, and like the bones of animals, they are alive. They deserve to be treated with respect. I try to walk gently.

I push Tutelo in front of me where I can watch her. Just ahead of her walks, Wrass. He has also seen eleven summers, but he's four moons older than I am —maybe the oldest boy here—and he's brave. My father says that Wrass is destined to be a great warrior. Tall for his age, he has a face like an eagle's, with sharp dark eyes and a hooked nose. Wrass can track better and shoot farther than any other boy in our village. I have always been jealous of Wrass. As the war chief's only son, much is expected of me, but

I have always been afraid. I am the boy who runs when the bear approaches. The boy who hurries home when darkness falls. And I've never been very good with a bow. Not like Wrass, who can shoot a bird out of the sky at fifty paces. For the first time in my life, I am grateful for his skills. My deepest hope is that he is waiting for his chance to grab a war club and start a fight that will allow a few of us to escape.

When he turns his head, and I see his profile, my hopes evaporate.

Wrass looks as lost and terrified as the rest of us. Every time one of the warriors glares at him, Wrass starts shaking.

Sunlight pierces the rain clouds and slants across the forest, casting geometric patterns upon the rocks. I let my head fall forward to stare at them, and my shoulder-length black hair hangs over the front of my buck-skin shirt. Some of the children have capes, but Tutelo and I scrambled from our beds so fast that we didn't have the chance to grab ours. Last night, when Big Man let us sleep for two hands of time, I curled my body around Tutelo to keep her warm, and dreamed of Mother leading a war party into the camp and killing Big Man and all of his warriors.

If I live to see one thousand summers, that dream will still be the best of my life.

Big Man leads us off the rocks and down a steep trail into a small clearing where he calls, "Make the children sit down."

Two warriors trot down the line swinging war clubs, forcing us to drop to the damp oak leaves. Tutelo tucks her hand into mine. Her fingers are icy cold. I lift them to blow on them, and she shivers at the sudden warmth.

"We're going to be all right. Just be quiet, Tutelo."

"Where's…" She stops herself from asking, and I clutch her hand and nod.

Only when I start looking around do I see that this small clearing has been used before. Holes have been scooped out of the leaves, as though many children slept here and covered themselves with the leaves for warmth. Fragments of a broken clay cup scatter the ground to my left. Beneath a fallen log, I see the top half of a girl's cornhusk doll.

Has Big Man brought other captive children here? Why?

Big Man gathers his warriors around him, and they whisper to each other, but I can't make out any of their words.

I look at the leaves, and my thoughts turn to those other children. I swear I can smell their last moments here. Fear sweat drifts on the air, and I pick up the faint coppery odor of blood. *What happened to you?*

Wrass seems to smell these things, as well. He lifts his hooked nose, scents the wind, and his mouth tightens.

Tutelo bites her lip, looks back and forth between us, and asks, "Where's Mother?"

The words are like spear thrusts to my belly. "Coming," I whisper. "She's coming."

"When?"

"Soon. She and Father are tracking us. It will take some time."

Tutelo heaves a deep sigh and leans her head against my shoulder.

At the head of the group, the three new girls start talking to each other.

Big Man says, "Quiet."

One of the girls says a last word to her friend, and Big Man shouts, "I said, *quiet!*"

Two of the girls sit as if frozen, staring wide-eyed at him, but the talkative girl says, "I just wanted to finish—"

Big Man stalks toward her, and the expression on his face makes my blood go cold. The blow is swift and fierce. The girl shrieks and topples backward. When she rolls onto her side, blood pours from her mouth and spatters the bright autumn leaves.

Big Man glares at the rest of us. "Do you understand now? See what happens if you make me angry? If you do not obey me instantly? Be *quiet!*"

The only sounds are the wind through the trees and the soft sobbing of the baby.

We seem to sit forever, staring at each other, staring at our captors. I am certain that every child is thinking the same thing I am: *Someone is coming for us. That's why we're here. This is a meeting place. Who is coming?*

In less than one hand of time, nine strangers appear. They are like ghosts floating out of the forest. One is a boy about my age. Seven of them are lean, hungry men with mean eyes. The tallest man moves like a gangly stork and carries a heavy hide pack slung over his shoulder. The last person is a woman. She is old, maybe forty summers. Graying black hair hangs in greasy twists around her wrinkled face, and her eyes...her eyes are black bottomless pits. She seems to have no souls. Her toothless mouth is puckered and hard, and her nose resembles a sun-withered plum. When she speaks, it is as though sandstone boulders are rubbing together. Each word is a scratchy blow: "Get them up. Let me look at them."

"Get up," Big Man orders. "All of you. Stand up. The great Gannajero wants to see you."

We stand. All of us are trembling. I have never heard of Gannajero, but it terrifies me that Big Man does not care if I know her name. It is as though he believes she is so powerful nothing can harm her.

Gannajero drags over the boy who came with her, shoves him into our group, then slowly walks down the line, scowling at each of us. When she looks at me, my legs go weak. Evil lives in her eyes. I can feel it coiling around my heart, squeezing the life from it. I can't breathe. When she moves on to the next child, I stagger and lock my knees to keep standing.

Wrass tries to be brave. He has his jaw clenched and stares back at her without blinking. This makes Gannajero smile at him. It is not a pleasant smile, but a promise of pain to come.

Crows squawk, and Gannajero looks up to watch them soar through the sky. It is a small flock, ten or twelve jet-black birds. In a hoarse voice, she cries, *"Caw! Caw,* caw!" The crows seem startled. As though curious, many of them cock their heads and began to circle above her, angling their wings, watching, and *thocking* inquisitively to each other.

Gannajero's mouth opens in a toothless smile, and she says, "Are any of you children related?"

The oldest of the three Flint girls answers, "We are sisters."

Agres says, "So are we."

I hesitate, not sure whether I should give her this information. Before I can respond, Tutelo says, "We are brother and sister."

Gannajero turns to Big Man and points at Agres. "Why did you bring that one? What use do I have for an infant?"

Big Man gestures awkwardly. "The girl refused to leave it. I thought it was easier to let her keep it for a while."

Agres' face goes white. She clutches her sister more tightly to her chest. Her gaze darts from Big Man to Gannajero. The terrible truth is dawning, but she doesn't believe it yet.

None of us do.

Gannajero walks back toward her warriors. As she passes Big Man, she says, "The baby is yours. I will take the others. Kotin, pay him."

The gangly warrior unslings his heavy pack, walks forward, and hands it to Big Man.

Big Man places the pack on the ground. When he opens it, awed whispers filter through the gathering. The pack is filled with exquisite strings of pearls, pounded sheets of copper, etched shell gorgets, and many things I cannot see. Enough wealth to ransom a village. Big Man chuckles and begins tossing shell gorgets and pendants to each of his friends. They grin and laugh. Broken Teeth does a little dance of joy.

Wrass glances at me, silently asking if I understand this. I shake my head.

I do not understand. Child slaves are not worth so much. A few strings of shell beads for each of us would be enough.

"I'll meet you again next moon. But not here," Gannajero says to Big Man. "I'll send a messenger to tell you where."

"Fine."

Gannajero turns to her warriors. "Bring all of them except the baby."

She trudges away into the forest, and her warriors circle us like a pack of hungry dogs. The tall, gangly man, Kotin, holds out his hands to Agres. "Be a good girl. Give me the child."

Agres bursts into tears. "No. She's just a baby!"

"I don't have time to play games. Give her to me."

Agres starts to back away, and this enrages Kotin. He lunges for Agres, grabs her arm, and flings her to the ground. She loses hold of her sister, and the baby bounces into the leaves, shrieking. Agres madly crawls for her sister, but before she can reach her, Kotin brutally kicks Agres in the ribs and sends her sprawling.

"My father is a chief! He's going to kill you!" Agres shouts.

Kotin picks up the bundled baby and tosses it to Big Man. "Gannajero said this was yours."

Big Man catches it. "What am I going to do with it?"

Kotin shrugs, glances at the wailing child, and says, "The rest of you. Follow me."

I grip Tutelo's hand and walk. The world is blurry.

"Get up," one of the warriors says to Agres.

She struggles to rise, but can't. She's crying too hard. "My father—" She chokes on the word. "He'll find you!"

"Yes, yes, I can't wait to meet him." The man acts as though he has heard these same words from hundreds of children. He drags Agres to her feet and forces her into line just ahead of Tutelo. She is clutching her ribs and groaning as though they are broken.

As Agres passes Big Man, she lunges, grabs the baby, and runs into the forest. Spontaneous cheers rise from the children. We are all praying she escapes. If she can do it…

Gannajero shouts, "Kotin, teach a lesson!"

Kotin unslings his bow and nocks an arrow. He takes his time sighting down the shaft.

Agres is still running when the arrow pierces her back. She careens forward, trying to keep hold of her sister, but it is too difficult. Blood is drenching her dress, pulsing in time to her heartbeat. She has only enough strength to gently place the baby on the ground, then stagger over to an oak trunk and lean against it.

Big Man and his warriors don't even seem to notice. They split up and trot away in different directions. No one looks back.

"Little fool," Gannajero says, and glares at the rest of us. "Look and learn. If you run, you die."

Gannajero tramps away. Her warriors force us to march up the trail behind her, but I keep looking back. For an eternity, Agres stands there. Finally, she sinks to her knees and collapses into the leaves without a sound.

For another finger of time, I hear the baby crying.

We turn onto a new trail and head down into a grove of pines. My heart is beating in my ears, slamming against my skull, growing louder and louder, until a stunned ringing shakes me.

Crows circle overhead, and I hear magpies in the distance. In a few days, there will be nothing left of Agres or her sister. Their bones will be picked clean, then covered by leaves, and finally melt into the forest floor. No one will know what happened to them.

I can't stop myself from wondering when the same thing is going to happen to Tutelo and me.

Our People believe that the dead must be buried properly or their afterlife souls cannot reach the Land of the Dead. Instead, it becomes a homeless ghost, wandering the forests alone, forever.

Don't think about it. Don't.

It's raining. I look up. Misty veils drift down from dark clouds. The forest begins to hiss, and the bright autumn leaves bob as they are patted by the drops.

Walk. Just keep walking.

3

As the campfires of the dead flashed between the clouds, they cast a dusty radiance over the rain-drenched forest, silvering the dark oaks and elms that covered the mountains. The muddy trail was awash. In the indigo shadows cast by the wind-touched branches, the water seemed to rise and fall like waves.

Sonon took a deep breath, allowing the pungent fragrances of earth and bark to seep into his exhausted body; then he twined his hands in the girl's long black hair and continued dragging her through the mud. His arms and back ached from the labor. In the constant downpour, he kept losing his hold.

As he walked, he softly sang, *"The crow comes, the crow comes, pity the little children, beat the drum..."*

With each step, he heard the beating of the crow's wings in his head. It was always there. A soft rhythmic pushing of air, as though she lived right behind his eyes, saw his world, knew his most precious dreams. He'd heard her wings since he'd seen six summers. Sometimes, especially at night, he felt her darkness pressing against his eyes like icy hands, trying to shove her way out of his skull.

"*...beat the drum, grab the young, and run, run, run.*"

He stopped to catch his breath and take a new grip. His gaze lowered to the girl's perfect oval face. In the flashes of lightning, her copper earspools blazed. He studied her turned-up nose and the unnatural angle of her gaping mouth. Her dark eyes were half-open, staring blankly at the mist that encircled the treetops. Mud coated her white doehide dress, making it cling to her body like a second skin, highlighting the contours of her young breasts and hips. He wiped his drenched face on his sleeve and let out a shaky breath.

It had been raining hard since nightfall, soaking the brittle forest and turning the paths into creeks. Fortunately, the runoff would cover his trail. As always, Sky Woman, the grandmother of human beings, had seen his honor, and chosen to protect him from his enemies—but it made his task much harder. Most of the day, he had carried her in his arms. Now, he could only manage to drag her.

"No," he whispered, and squeezed his eyes closed for several long moments. "We are almost home. I owe her more than this."

Despite his fatigue, he steadied his muscles and bent to slip his arms beneath her to carry her again. It wasn't much farther. He could do this. He lifted her and slogged on down the trail, drowning in the sensation of her stone-cold body pressed tightly against his. Her long hair draped his left arm and stuck wetly to his thigh. Every step he took, those dark strands shimmered, and he longed to weep.

For a time, he just listened to the clicking of her shell bracelets and tried to fight back the memories.

A short while after she'd fallen, he'd gone to her. She'd stared up at him. The silent pleading in her dark eyes had left him trembling.

Blessed Creator, how many times had girls gazed at him like that? How many times had he knelt in their blood and lifted their wounded bodies into his arms? He was a warrior and supposed to be hardened to such things...but he doubted he ever would be.

Lightning flashed, and Thunderers dove right over his head. He gasped, and in the sudden glare of brilliantly lit oaks, he felt somehow unreal...more like a ghost walking through the Land of the Dead than through lands belonging to the People of the Standing Stone.

As the Thunderers cracked and soared away, a

gust of wind rattled the branches. Showers of wet leaves cascaded down around him. Sonon shivered. Already, the nights were colder. It would not be long now until Hatho, the Frost Spirit, came again to live among humans. Hatho was an old man in white who carried a large club that he used to strike against the trees, to make them creak and crack as the icy winds of winter descended upon the world.

Gathering his strength, Sonon forced himself to breathe.

The night scents smelled incredibly clear to him. The tang of damp oaks mixed sweetly with the fragrances of the nearby Forks River and the earthiness of the thunderstorm that seemed to have no end.

Ahead, through the dense tangle of trees, he glimpsed the shell midden used by the People of the Hills. The midden—a trash mound three times the height of a man—marked their territorial border. In a few paces, he would be out of Standing Stone country.

Just the thought filled him with hope. He forced his shaking legs to move faster. The girl's body rocked in his arms.

"Just a little longer," he murmured to her.

Repeated flashes of lightning turned the shell midden into a wildly twinkling hill.

As he started up the steep slope, he stumbled, almost dropped her, and clutched her to his broad chest. "Careful," he hissed, more to himself than to her. "Careful now. We are almost there."

With his sandals skidding and clattering on the wet shells, he carried her to the top of the mound and gently lowered her body. The view from up here was gorgeous. Whitecaps glistened down the length of the wide Forks River, and for as far as he could see, lightning slashed the stormy sky.

"You're home," he said, and bent to stroke her face. Her skin felt cold and clammy.

Sonon straightened. For a few brief instants, he did not hear the rain or the wind through the branches. His souls were filled with a terrible silence. Each person, before he crossed the bridge to the afterlife, had to discover what he was running from and why. This moment—this exact moment—was the heartbeat of his own search. The terror that had stalked him all his life.

"The crow comes, the crow comes, beat the drum, hide the young, and run, run, run," he sang as he tried to focus his eyes. A dark fluttering filled his head. The iron-gray night was suddenly broken and shimmering, as though each instant was nothing more than a shattered glimpse of death.

Desperation tingled his veins.

He lifted his face to the storm... The rain washed her blood from his hands... The roar of Thunderers drowned his agonized cries.

When he could breathe again, he choked out the words, "One f-final task."

He grabbed the leather cord of his gorget and lifted his precious conch shell pendant from around his neck. The False Face image carved into the shell stared up at him with hollow eyes. Holding it in both hands, he breathed his soul into it, then placed it upon her chest, right over the protruding shaft of the arrow. As he straightened, the old, tarnished, copper beads that encircled the collar of his cape clicked together.

"When I reach the bridge to the afterlife, remember me," he whispered.

He watched the cascades of falling leaves that showered the forest while he thought about death: hers and his own. There was a bridge that spanned a black abyss of nothingness, and each soul had to cross it to reach the afterlife. Standing on this side of the bridge were all the animals a man had known in his life. Those he had helped defended him and gave him the time to cross the bridge. Those he had hurt chased him, trying to make him fall into the abyss, where his soul would float in black emptiness for eternity. On the opposite side of the bridge —if a man was going to make it—he saw all the people he'd ever loved, waiting for him. A man who was not going to make it across saw nothing.

Sonon knew, for he had stood upon the bridge many times and seen across the border of death to what lay beyond. That emptiness still lived in his dreams, calling to him in a lover's voice, luring him to step onto the planks. Someday he would freely walk into those open arms and never return. He longed for that black peace with all his heart.

Cold wind rustled the trees around him, and leaves pirouetted through the air.

He sucked several deep breaths into his lungs and forced his trembling legs down the midden slope toward the trail that led east.

4

Gonda pulled his elk-hide cape more tightly around his muscular shoulders. Sunlight penetrated the forest in bars and streaks of fallow gold, but there was no warmth to it. He was a slender man with a round face and heavy brow. He had seen twenty-six summers pass, but this morning he felt older than the forests. As he knelt to examine a washed-out track in the trail, his short black hair fell forward.

"What are you?" he whispered. "Nothing?"

The scuff mark was frost-rimmed and skimmed with ice. It could have been made by anything—a deer, a man, even a raccoon. He vented a frustrated breath and rose to his feet.

Buttonbush thickets crowded the spaces between the towering sycamores and shorter sassafras trees. Birds perched among the branches, plucking at the few shriveled fruits that clung to the leafless red stalks. A riot of sparrow and wren songs filled the air.

He expelled a breath and propped his fists on his hips.

At dawn, he'd found dim marks at the edges of the flooded trail, as though a man had been dragging a heavy pack through the water and, occasionally, the pack had scooped up mud. But the marks had vanished over one hand of time ago. In desperation, both of them had kept pushing onward up the same trail, hoping to spot more sign, but so far, they'd seen nothing certain.

After two days, this was the most promising trail they'd found—if it was a trail—and every instant they delayed, every moment they spent discussing what they should do next, their enemy was getting farther and farther away.

Gonda glanced at his former wife, Koracoo. She stood five paces behind him, examining something on the forest floor. He kept praying she would look up and meet his gaze, perhaps smile at him, anything to keep him going. She did not.

They had been married for twelve summers—until two days ago when she'd set his belongings outside the charred husk of their longhouse and told him to go home to his own clan.

He stepped off the trail and continued his search through the trees.

Blessed gods, couldn't she see that his own guilt was strangling him? Even if they found their children alive and well, he would never forgive himself. The images of burning longhouses and dead friends would remain open wounds on his souls for as long as he lived.

Gonda stopped, seeing a curious shape just beneath the overhanging branches of a bush. He bent over, frowned at it, and called, "Koracoo? You'd better come look at this."

She lifted her head. At twenty-seven summers, Koracoo was unusually tall for a woman, twelve hands. She'd chopped her black hair short in mourning. It created a jagged frame for her beautiful face. Since the destruction of their village, her large dark eyes maintained an almost perpetually stunned expression. Over her knee-length war shirt, she wore a red cape. In the middle of the cape, the blue painting of a buffalo defiantly stared out. "Are you sure?"

"I've been a warrior for thirteen summers, Koracoo. Don't you think I know how to recognize a man's track?"

As Koracoo walked toward him, sunlight gilded the copper inlay in her war club, giving it an edge of flame. It had a name, that club: *Corpse-Eye*. His own nameless club was made of fire-hardened oak. Hers was a wood no one had ever seen before—dark, dense, and old. Legend said that CorpseEye had once belonged to Sky Woman herself. Strange images were carved on the shaft: antlered wolves, winged tortoises, and prancing buffalo. A red quartzite cobble was tied to the top of the club, making it a very deadly weapon—one Koracoo wielded with great expertise. She constantly polished CorpseEye with walnut oil, as her father had done, and his father before him, and his before him, back into the obscure mists of time.

Koracoo stopped beside him. "Show me."

Gonda held the brush aside for her.

As she knelt to scrutinize the frost-rimmed track, the lines around her eyes deepened.

He watched her. More than anything, he longed to touch her, to lie in her arms and talk about his mistakes until he could bear them. He was the father of her children. Between them was the unbreakable bond of two people who had seen their children stolen away to a fate neither of them dared imagine. Only in her arms would he ever find comfort.

But as the days passed, it seemed less and less likely. On the rare occasions when she looked at him now, it was with the eyes of a cold, impatient stranger.

Koracoo said, "He wore finely woven cornhusk sandals. A wealthy man. A man of status."

"Yes. Let's go. We're wasting precious time."

"I need to study this a little longer." She kept her eyes on the sandal print.

Gonda grumbled under his breath. Every tendon in his body was stretched taut, telling him to leave, to keep searching. But she was war chief, and he was deputy. She made the decisions.

He scowled at the track. The herringbone pattern of the sandal weave was distinctive, woven by the Hills People. There were five kinds of People south of Skanodario Lake: Flint People, the People of the Landing, People of the Mountain, People of the Hills, and their own tribe of Standing Stone People. The People of the Hills had the most warriors and the largest villages. They were—despite what the Standing Stone People wished to believe—the greatest power in the land.

Koracoo said, "He was a Hills warrior."

"Yes. Probably a big, heavy man, because his feet sank deeply into the mud."

Her eyes narrowed in thought before she replied, "Or he was carrying a heavy load."

"Maybe."

Koracoo stood, and her gaze moved to the shell midden partially visible through the tangle of tree trunks. The mound glittered with frost. Canassatego Village, a Hills People village, had used the same trash site for ten summers; it was huge, covered with freshwater mussel shells, broken pottery, ashes from their fires, and other refuse.

"His toes pointed toward the midden," Koracoo observed.

"Yes. So?"

"Let's see if he came here alone, or met someone. You go left of the trail. I'll go right." When she turned to look at him to make sure he understood, his heartbeat stilled. Her eyes were as black and translucent as obsidian, and cut just as keenly. "I'll meet you at the midden." Koracoo stepped away.

Gonda went left. It took another half-hand of time before they reached the base of the mound. It stood three times the height of a man. As Elder Brother Sun climbed higher into the sky, the layer of ice began to melt, leaving the wet shells glistening like river rocks.

"Another track," Koracoo called, and pointed at the ground.

Gonda worked his way over to her and stared down at the place where the man's sandals had skidded off the shells, heaping them into small piles.

There were several more such piles all the way up the midden slope. At this time of the morning, each cast a shadow. "He was careful until he got here; then he started rushing. See where he slipped?"

"Yes."

"Stay here," she ordered. "I'll see if there is anything on top of the midden."

"Koracoo, please, let me do it. You will be a perfect target standing alone at the top. There may be enemy warriors watching from the trees. I am more expendable than you are."

"Stay here." She started up the slope.

Gonda kept his gaze on her. She was moving slowly, climbing, studying, climbing. Since the attack on Yellowtail Village and the loss of their children, he panicked whenever she was out of his sight.

She's all right. Leave it be.

They had faced so many hardships together. Behind them were burned villages, friends long dead, and young dreams smothered beyond all recall. He knew her better than she knew herself... and she him. Why couldn't she forgive him?

His practiced warrior's gaze moved over the forest, searching for odd colors or shapes—anything that would reveal a hidden enemy—then darted back to Koracoo. She was almost to the mound top.

In the sky above her, twenty or more ravens soared, their wings flashing in the sunlight. Such large flocks were a common sight these days. Whenever people went to war, they did not go alone. Carrion eaters followed them, waiting their turns to feast.

"There's a body up here," Koracoo called.

Gonda's eyes widened. He glanced at the ravens again. He should have known. "A body?

That must be what he was dragging. Male or female? Can you tell?"

Koracoo walked to the edge of the mound and gestured for him to come to her, but added, "Don't disturb the tracks."

Gonda veered wide and hurried up the opposite side of the slope. Long before he reached the top, he could smell the stench of rotting human flesh. Then he saw the girl lying on her back. The birds had pecked out her eyes and devoured most of the flesh of her face. Worse, wolves had been at her belly. Ropes of half-chewed intestines snaked across the shells. The broken shaft of an arrow protruded from her chest.

Gonda gestured to the arrow. "He was a good shot. That's straight through the heart."

"Or he was close." Koracoo swung CorpseEye up and rested the club on her shoulder. The red quartzite cobble glinted. "Her clothing marks her as one of the Hills People, and look at her jewelry."

"Yes, I see."

Shell bracelets encircled the gnawed wrists, and beautiful copper earspools decorated the girl's lobes. An elaborately carved conch shell pendant lay a short distance away. It was gorgeous: A False Face with a long bent nose, slanted mouth, and hollow eyes stared up from the shell. The False Face Spirits who inhabited such masks could cure illness. Had the dead girl been ill? The leather thong had probably been chewed through by the wolves and the pendant dragged off.

Gonda walked closer and searched the area around the mangled corpse for any clues that might reveal her killer. The longer he studied the body, the more unease he felt.

Koracoo clenched her fist around CorpseEye. "She is not one of our children."

"No. Do you think we're on the wrong trail?"

"It's possible, but many villages have been attacked in the past few days. She may have been herded into a group of captives that included our children."

"Child slavery is an ugly part of warfare, but it—"

"This was not warfare," Koracoo said.

"What do you mean?"

Koracoo used CorpseEye to point. "If she'd been killed by enemy warriors, they would have taken that magnificent jewelry."

Gonda looked at the copper earspools again. Even now, though he'd have to pull them through rotting flesh, they'd be worth a fortune in trade. "I didn't think of that."

Koracoo walked around the other side of the body. "And no enemy warrior would have carried her up here to the top of this mound. He would have left her where she fell. Who would go to the effort of carrying a dead girl to the top of a trash mound?"

"A man who wanted to make a point."

Koracoo straightened. She had an oval face with full lips and a small, narrow nose. "What point?"

"That she was filth? Or refuse? Perhaps her killer hated her."

Koracoo thoughtfully gazed out at the Forks River. "Or perhaps he loved her. The view from up here is beautiful. I can see halfway across the Hills People country." She studied the body again and softly said, "All we know with fair certainty is that she was carried up here by one of her own people."

Gonda used the toe of his moccasin to smooth out a ridge of shells. "Should we keep following this trail? Or go back and start over at Yellowtail Village?"

Koracoo tensed. "This is still the best trail we've found. The only trail. I say we follow it wherever it leads."

He exhaled a breath and nodded. "I agree. Which direction should we go? Do we follow him to the west? Or do we backtrack him to the east and hope we find the place the girl was killed? If we find him, he may be able to answer all of our questions."

"If he chooses to, which I doubt."

"There are ways to 'encourage' his cooperation."

Koracoo shook her head. "That will take even more time and may be fruitless."

Gonda flapped his arms against his sides. "Then I say we backtrack him. If we can find where the girl was killed, it may answer just as many of our questions."

Koracoo didn't respond, and he knew what she must be thinking. At this very moment, their clan elders would be salvaging what they could from the charred remains of Yellowtail Village, burying the dead, and trying to decide what to take with them. Though the elders had sanctioned their search for the missing children, they expected Koracoo and Gonda to be home soon to help defend the survivors as they marched to Bur Oak Village, a Standing Stone village five days away.

"What do you think we should do?" he asked. "We haven't much time."

Her gaze drifted over the crimson-hued forest before she said, "We backtrack him. If the trail goes cold, or it becomes clear it has nothing to do with our lost children, we will go home."

"Agreed."

Koracoo headed down the midden trail, and Gonda turned to look at the False Face pendant. He walked over, picked it up, and tucked it into his belt pouch.

As he trotted to catch up with Koracoo, melting ice began to drip out of the trees and shower the forest floor. Gonda flipped up the hood of his buckskin cape and shivered.

The morning was warming up, releasing the brittle scents of autumn, and he wanted to enjoy it for as long as he could. He had known Koracoo his entire life. While they could not track in the darkness, for the next few days there would be no real rest. From dawn until dusk, they would be searching the ground and brush. They would eat and drink on the run. At night, they would take turns sleeping. One of them would always be standing guard.

The faces of Tutelo and Odion smiled at him from his memories, and he had to fight back the cry that rose in his throat.

Deep inside him, a voice kept repeating, *My fault. All my fault.*

He focused his eyes on Koracoo's back and tried to think only of her.

5

Gonda had not had a sip of water all day. Since dawn he had been moving, walking up and down the twisting mountain trails, searching for any sign that a man carrying a girl had passed this way. Now, in the late afternoon, he was desperately thirsty. But it did not matter. Off and on all day, they had found the sign: a broken branch along the trail, a fragment of white doe-hide caught on brush, partial tracks, and drag marks. This *was* the trail of the man who had carried the girl to the midden. The problem was that they still did not know if this trail had anything to do with their missing children. For all they knew, they could be wasting their time while Odion, Tutelo, and Wrass were being sold from one Trader to another. It would not be long until the children's trail went stone cold.

Gonda studied the trees. The damp chestnut limbs stood starkly against the sunlight. Here and there, fallen nuts dotted the ground. He reached down, picked up several, and tucked them into his belt pouch for later when...

A strange sound whispered through the forest.

Almost...eerie. He heard Koracoo coming up the trail and held up a hand to stop her. She went deathly silent, listening, as he was.

The sound came again. Leaves rustled, but not with the wind.

Gonda pulled an arrow from the quiver on his back and nocked it in his bow; then he used it to point in the direction of the sound.

A soft hiss told Gonda that Koracoo, too, had nocked an arrow in her bow. After another five heartbeats, Koracoo eased up beside him. Her dark eyes were intent, focused on the source of the sound in the forest ahead.

They stood in silence, both studying the lay of the land, searching for hidden foes. He led the way, warily heading toward the sound.

In another thirty paces, they walked into a small clearing fringed by gigantic oaks. Gonda's eyes narrowed. Someone had been here recently. The deep autumn leaves that blanketed the grass had been scooped into odd shapes, as though many people had shoved them aside to sit down, perhaps to build fires.

"What is this?" Koracoo whispered.

He shook his head uncertainly.

Sunset sheathed the forest, glittering from the tallest pines like a fine paint made of ground amber. A luminous wall of Cloud People crowded the sky to the north.

"Smell anything?" he asked.

Koracoo flared her nostrils and shook her head. "No."

Gonda nodded. There was no smell of smoke. If someone had camped here, he would have built a fire to warm himself and cook his food. As warriors, they'd raided and burned enough villages to know how long it took for the stench to fade.

A tingle climbed Gonda's spine. None of this made sense. He needed a few moments to think and motioned for Koracoo to take cover. She stepped behind a tree trunk two paces away.

Gonda hid behind one of the many lichen-covered boulders that thrust up across the mountains.

Sunset had just begun to purple the western horizon, and the eagle shadows that played in the trees had a vaguely lavender hue. Otherwise, the only movement was the faint breeze through the branches.

The sound...leaves moving?

His gut knotted.

Blessed gods, what is that?

Anxious, almost to the point of carelessness, Gonda clenched his bow so hard his fingertips went white. He forced himself to think. They'd been tracking the man all day and had seen none of the refuse that inevitably marked the trails of warriors. It was as though the man had simply grabbed the dead girl and headed toward the shell midden without stopping. Why would anyone do that? Had he known the girl? A relative would have taken her home and buried her properly, so that her afterlife soul could find its way to the Land of the Dead. Or...had he been afraid to take her home? Would his village have punished him?

Koracoo hissed to get his attention and used her nocked arrow to point at something beneath a fallen log.

His gaze searched the area until he saw what appeared to be part of a child's toy—a cornhusk doll.

"Koracoo, you circle north; I'll veer south."

She nodded and slipped into the forest shadows.

Gonda carefully stepped off the trail and started moving through the deep leaves. His moccasins crackled softly. Every two steps, he halted to listen. As Cloud People drifted across the face of Elder Brother Sun, shadows darkened the trees, then vanished as the amber gleam again flooded the forest.

He swerved around a small outcrop of granite boulders...heard again a whisper of leaves moving... and forced himself to look at the clearing. To *see*. If there was someone out there, he should be able to make out an odd color, or shape, perhaps a glimpse of clothing. He saw nothing but strange dips and humps in the leafbed.

Across the meadow, Koracoo's shadow slipped through the trees, cautiously approaching the clearing from the north.

Gonda let his gaze drift around the forest. Were there warriors hiding out there, just waiting for someone, anyone, to come to the sound? Was this a clever trap?

Koracoo signaled for him to stop.

He rubbed his mouth with the back of his hand while he waited. He hadn't heard whatever it was that had spooked her.

Koracoo took two more steps through the trees on the north end of the clearing. Then she said, "Gonda? Come here. This may be where the girl died."

Gonda trotted to meet her. For a time, they did not speak; they just looked at the blood that soaked the oak trunk.

"How old do you think that blood is?"

Koracoo slung her bow and knelt. "Two days. Three, maybe. You can see where the mice have been chewing at the soaked bark."

She began slowly pulling away the leaves at the base of the tree.

When she neared the ground level, the leaves were stuck together with old blood. She gently lifted the clumps and set them aside, looking for more.

"A sandal track." She tapped it with her finger.

Gonda moved forward and bent to examine it. "A big man. Heavy. Or perhaps he'd already lifted the girl into his arms when this track was made."

"Yes." Koracoo's dark brows pinched over her small nose. She scowled at the track for several moments. "Don't you think it's odd that he's wearing sandals? It's late autumn. He should be wearing moccasins."

"Maybe he's an idiot?"

"Or maybe sandals are all he has, but..."

Koracoo tilted her head, and Gonda saw that she was listening again—listening as though their lives depended upon it. He held his breath.

In a clipped voice, Koracoo said, "Do you hear it?"

A few paces away, the leaves whispered.

Gonda braced himself. "Yes."

Hope swelled fit to burst his chest. They both straightened, and their eyes focused on the leaves. They fluttered. "You go," he said. "I'll cover you with my bow."

Koracoo moved forward on cat feet. The leaves continued to flutter as if from shallow rhythmic puffs of air. Breathing? His heart tightened.

Koracoo crouched down, brushed away leaves, then stopped. In an agonized voice, she said, "Oh, no," and reached both hands deep into the leaves to pull out a tightly wrapped bundle.

"What is it?" Gonda rushed forward.

"It's a baby." Koracoo slumped to the ground and cradled the child in her left arm while she frantically pulled the blanket from its face with her right hand.

Gonda kept glancing up at the forest, his bow still drawn. When he looked down again, a small pale face, framed with black hair, shone within the blanket. The child's dark eyes were slitted, the lids fluttering as though it was just barely alive. "It's a miracle that the child didn't freeze to death. The Forest Spirits must have protected it."

"If we don't act quickly, the Forest Spirits' efforts will have been for naught."

Koracoo rested the baby in her lap, jerked her cape over her head, and pulled open the laces of her war shirt. For a brief moment, he glimpsed her breasts, and it comforted him.

"What are you doing?" he asked.

"Warming her." Koracoo peeled off the child's soiled sack—revealing that it was a girl—and tossed the sack into the leaves; then she tucked the baby down the front of her war shirt. "Blessed gods, she's freezing."

"Koracoo...we can't take her with us. You know that, don't you?"

"If I stand up, can you slip my cape over my head and tie it beneath the baby?"

Gonda slung his bow and picked up Koracoo's cape. "Yes, but—"

"I'm aware of the problem, Gonda." Carefully holding the child against her, she got to her feet.

Gonda slipped her cape over her head and then pulled the ends up and tied them around Koracoo's waist to form a kind of sling for the baby inside her brown shirt.

"Tighter," Koracoo said. "If I have to fight, I want to be able to use my hands to swing my club."

Gonda complied, retying the ends as tightly as he could. "If you understand the problem, why are you—?"

"We have to find the nearest village. Fast. This child needs food and shelter. Her afterlife soul is already out wandering the forest, about to leave her body.

Gonda peered at the soiled sack. "The red-and-black spirals mark her as one of the People of the Hills, probably Hawk Clan. If that doesn't slap some sense into you, I don't know what will."

"The nearest Hills village is Atotarho Village."

Among the Hills People, when a chief died, his clan matron, in consultation with the other women of the clan, selected the new chief, and he was given the name of the deceased man. The new chief was then "raised up," and the dead chief, thereby, "resuscitated." If the new chief proved unworthy of his position, he could be "dehorned," and his name taken away. Villages always took the name of their chief, and Chief Atotarho was no friend of theirs.

Gonda said, "Atotarho is an evil sorcerer. We can't go there. None of us, including the baby, will survive."

The Hills People were their sworn enemies. In fact—though he couldn't be sure—there may have been Atotarho warriors with the Mountain warriors who had attacked Yellowtail Village and taken their children. The Hills and Mountain Peoples were allies and often combined forces to assault Standing Stone villages.

"We don't have a choice, Gonda."

"Of course we have a choice. She's not one of our people. We can leave her here."

The expression on Koracoo's face went straight to his heart. Granted, she had just lost her children in a raid and didn't know if they were alive or dead, but the way she clutched the baby against her made no sense. They could *not* take it with them.

"I can't leave her to die," she said sternly. "Let's go."

Koracoo started to walk past him, and he grabbed her arm in a hard grip. "No! If you and I are captured or killed, *our* children may be lost forever. Leave the baby here! It's almost dead. Leave it."

Koracoo shook off his grip and glared at him, but he saw bone-deep pain in her eyes. "Very well. We'll split up. You keep following this trail. As soon as I've found a safe place where the baby will be cared for, I'll catch up with you."

He shook his head as though he hadn't heard right. "I'm not going to let you walk into a Hills village alone. If they kill you on sight, I'll never forgive myself." He held out his arms. "Give me the child. I'll take it away, and you won't even have to watch."

The baby mewed, barely audible, and Koracoo's expression turned to stone. "Gonda, you can either keep following this trail, or come with me. Either way, we're losing the light."

Gonda exhaled hard. Arguing more would be futile. He threw up his hands in frustration, and said, "I'll go with you, but you're insane."

"Fine. You lead."

He checked the sunlight, nocked his bow again, and headed west. The deep leaves made it impossible to walk quietly. Even though wet, they shished and crackled beneath his moccasins. Behind him, he could hear Koracoo speaking gently to the child, telling it not to be afraid, that everything was going to be all right—which he seriously doubted.

Over his shoulder, he said, "And you'd better hide CorpseEye somewhere. Everyone knows that club and wants it. They'll steal it for sure."

"I will."

He'd taken another ten steps when he came to a deep pile of leaves. He kicked his way through them, launching several wet clumps high into the air...and stopped dead in the trail. Hot blood surged through his veins, and he suddenly felt light-headed.

In a shaking voice, he said, "Koracoo?"

"What?"

He aimed his bow at the bare patch of ground. "Look."

It had been raining that day. Dozens of small feet had sunken into the mud and the imprints had been preserved when the ground had frozen. Later, leaves had blown over the top.

Gonda whispered, "It is...isn't it?"

Koracoo came up beside him, saw the tracks, and sucked in a sudden breath. For the first time in days, she looked directly at him, and their gazes locked. He saw panic in her eyes to match his own. For a few brief instants, they shared their fear and grief, and he could finally get a full breath into his lungs.

Koracoo knelt, brushed at the leaves, and scrutinized the tracks. "Don't get your hopes up. It's definitely the trail of a group of children, but we have no way of knowing whether they are our children or not."

"Nonetheless, we should follow this trail now. Surely you know that. Forget the baby!"

Koracoo hesitated. Her eyes clung to the small moccasin prints in the mud. Then the baby let out a soft cry, and she squeezed her eyes closed.

"You know I'm right," he said. "Our children are worth more. I wish we didn't have to make a choice, but we do."

In the tawny halo of the light, her beautiful, tormented face seemed to be carved of amber. After five more heartbeats, she finally opened her eyes and rose to her feet.

"No, Gonda. I'm taking the child to Atotarho Village, but I'll be back here by dawn tomorrow. I'll catch up with you."

She slogged through the deep leaves and started up the trail.

Gonda stood for several moments staring at the tracks with his heart bursting in his chest. He could see his children's faces and hear their voices calling out to him, *"Father, where are you? You're coming for us, aren't you?"*

The pain in his chest was suffocating.

He opened and closed his fists. When he could stand it no longer, he tore his gaze away from their trail and stumbled backward, breathing hard.

It took another ten heartbeats before he could order his legs to trot after Koracoo.

6
ODION

A baby cries.

I lift my hands and cover my ears. The wail seems to seep through my skin and drifts on the pine-sharp winds that swirl old leaves up into the oak boughs before blowing them away through the chill golden afternoon. Why can't I get the cries of Agres' sister out of my heart?

Tutelo sleeps in the dead grass beside me. I keep glancing at her. Worrying. We are all shaky from the days of marching without food. We have rarely been on a trail. Usually we march through the trackless forests, meadows, or over rocks, which has made the travel even more exhausting. Today our guards ordered Tutelo and me to climb through trees, then across an outcrop of eroding granite where stunted saplings grew as thickly as river reeds. It took two hands of time. I don't know where the other children were at the time. Gannajero has assigned each of us a guard during the day. The guard can take us wherever he wishes if he arrives at dusk in the prearranged location. Often, the men carry us on their backs so they can travel faster.

I look around.

The camp is large. Many warriors have come to see Gannajero. But these men did not bring children to sell. They came to gamble. Fifteen men sit around a small fire, playing the stone game. There are three teams, each composed of five players. The gangly warrior, Kotin, holds a round wooden bowl. Six plum pits clack inside the dish. The pits are gaming pieces, ground to an oval shape, then burned black on one side and painted white on the other. He shakes the bowl and tosses the stones across an elk hide spread over the cold ground. Whoops and cheers go up from his friends, and howls of dismay from the strangers. Kotin throws his head back and laughs as he pulls in the glittering pile of stone knives, hide scrapers, and copper jewelry. The new warriors grumble and cast evil looks at Gannajero's team.

The wealth being won and lost stuns me, and I wonder if they are not wagering on more than tangles of necklaces and stone tools.

My eyes move to where the old woman sits alone in the middle of the clearing. Her head is back. She stares up at a flock of crows drifting on the wind currents above her. Her breath frosts as she speaks to the birds and makes strange signs in the air with a black feather. Is Gannajero performing some evil magical ritual? Or just praying for the Crows to bring her team good luck?

When we made camp two hands of time ago, she pulled aside the three Flint girls and forced them to put on beautiful doeskin dresses. Then she carefully combed and braided their hair. The elaborate red-and-yellow porcupine quillwork on their dresses flashes when they move. The girls kneel together twenty paces from the game, whispering.

I am the only Yellowtail child awake. I roll to my back and study the bare oak branches. The farther east we go, the fewer leaves there are, and the colder the nights become.

I am feverish and sick to my stomach all the time. I think it's the baby. Her cries are often so loud I cannot hear anything else. I swear her soul is inside me. I have glimpsed it, flitting behind my eyes like blue falling stars.

Her soul is flying. I feel it. It is the flight of the alone to the *Alone.*

At the game, Gannajero's men leap to their feet and shake their fists. Kotin has lost, and passes the bowl to the next team.

The baby shrieks inside me. I glance around, terrified.

"Stop crying!" I whisper. "Please, stop crying."

I must have spoken too loudly. The other boy,

who sleeps to my right, rolls over and stares at me. His brow furrows. He appears to be my age: eleven or twelve summers. He has a starved face—all the bones stick out—and hollow brown eyes. His flat nose and big ears make him resemble a bat. He is lucky, for he wears a heavy moosehide cape with the fur turned inside for warmth.

I whisper, "What's your name?"

I just barely hear him say, "Hehaka."

"I am Odion."

Wrass wakes and looks at us, then glances around to make sure our guards are both paying attention to the game before he crawls over to me. His beaked nose glows orange in the firelight. Dirty black hair frames his narrow face. His mouth is moving. He's trying to tell me something.

"I can't hear you, Wrass." The baby's cries drown out his words.

He crawls closer, cups a hand to my ear, and I feel his warm breath, but I hear nothing.

"I'm sorry, Wrass. I can't hear right now."

Hehaka mouths, *What's wrong with him?*

Wrass pushes back slightly, blinks at me, and looks around again, studying the guards. Both men are smiling at the game.

Wrass turns my head to look at my right ear, then my left, and he frowns. Very slowly, his mouth forms the words, *We...* then a word I don't understand...*run.*

I shake my head. "We can't run! There are too

many of them. They will just hunt us down and kill us, like they did Agres."

Wrass clenches his jaw. He looks desperate. He tries again, very slowly. *We...need...plan.*

Plan. Not run. *We need a plan.*

I prop myself up on one elbow and whisper, "Tell me what you're thinking."

Wrass stretches out beside me in the grass with his back to Hehaka. He clearly doesn't trust him. Hehaka gets the message and crawls away. Wrass waits until he's gone before he says, "...don't like him. He...Gannajero."

He came with Gannajero?

I can tell Wrass is terrified, but courage shines behind the terror. Faintly, I hear him say, "We...can't...too long, or we won't...find...way home."

I try to make myself fill in the words I can't hear: We can't wait too long, or we won't be able to find our way home?

I nod. "We should try to—"

Wrass suddenly jerks to look at the fire, and I see the men rising. The winners slap each other on the backs. The losers scowl and walk away.

Out in the clearing, Gannajero rises. Her hunched back makes her resemble a buffalo walking on its hind legs. She goes over to the three girls, and as she leans over them, her greasy twists of graying hair sway in their faces. She uses the black feather to stab at their chests. The girls nod.

The winning team of five men circle the girls like a pack of starving wolves, and smile. One of the girls is shaking badly.

The team leader—a skinny man wearing a black shirt—hands over the heavy bag of his winnings, Gannajero takes it, gestures to the girls, and walks away to examine her payment.

The three Flint girls rise as though they've been told to and huddle together.

One of the girls starts crying when she is dragged from the group. The man does not even try to hide his brutality. He slaps the girl, forces her to walk to a tree, and undress. When she is standing naked in the firelight, he shoves her against the trunk. He pulls up his warshirt, spits on his hard shaft, and thrusts himself inside her. She screams. Her mouth is wide, her pretty face twisted in shock. She tries to fight, and two warriors grab her arms and pin them. The last two men pick out their own girls.

My gaze jerks back to Wrass. His jaw is clenched so hard that his head is trembling. Rage lights his dark eyes. His fists are working, opening and closing as though gripping imaginary war clubs.

The other two Flint girls are thrown to the ground, and the men fall upon them. One flails her arms and tries to kick her attacker, but he slaps her into submission. The other girl lies limply, as though dead.

When the man who has the girl against the tree

finishes, he pulls away and another man takes his place.

Wrass' expression suddenly slackens, as though in understanding.

And then I understand, too.

Gannajero is a Trader. But she Trades in things men would be killed for in their own villages. These are children, not women. To couple with a girl before she exits the Women's House is considered the most insidious of crimes. Only incest with a child is worse. If a man forced a girl to couple with him in any village in the country, he would be hunted down and murdered.

But here in the wilderness, they simply have to pay enough.

Hehaka glances at the men, and then crawls back over. As though my ears have opened up, I clearly hear him say, "Sometimes the men want boys. You should be ready. They're going to hurt you."

"Tonight?" Wrass asks.

Hehaka shrugs. "I don't know. Maybe."

There is a tornado building inside Wrass. I see it spinning, forming. His dark eyes have a wet, savage glitter. He seems to sense my agony. He says, "Hehaka is just guessing. How could he know that?"

Hehaka crawls closer and whispers, "I know. Believe me. There are a few men who keep coming back just for me."

The pride in his voice shakes me to the bones.

"What do they make you do?" Wrass asks.

"Sometimes they just want to lie with me. Other times, they burn me with sticks, or they tie me up and cut my flesh with stone knives. See these scars?" He pulls up his sleeves, and Wrass and I gape at the white lines that crisscross his tanned skin. I swear there are hundreds of them, small and thin. Some appear to be punctures.

Wrass licks his lips nervously. "What's the matter with you? Why don't you run away?"

Hehaka pulls his sleeves down. "I've run away many times. The old woman always finds me and brings me back. Once, about four moons ago, I tried to kill myself." He turns so that we can see the scar that slashes his neck. "I took a chert flake and ripped open the big artery in my throat."

I shrink away from Hehaka, but Wrass leans closer for a good look. "Why didn't you die? You should have bled to death in a few hundred heartbeats."

"Yes, but she's a witch. She stopped my bleeding with a wave of her hand; then she turned herself into a crow and flew out into the forest. She found my wandering afterlife soul and shoved it back in my body. She won't let me die."

I start swallowing convulsively. A thin wail is leaching up through my lungs…

Tutelo's cold hand snakes through the grass and grasps mine. I did not know until this moment that she was awake. I feel as if my insides are melting. I whisper, "I'm right here, Tutelo."

"Odion? I—I'm afraid."

I squeeze her hand. "Try to sleep. We need to rest as much as we can, so we're strong enough to fight them when Mother and Father get here to rescue us."

Hehaka snickers at this, and Wrass grabs him by the hair and punches him solidly on the mouth.

Hehaka shrieks and scrambles away. Our guards turn. In a bored voice, Ugly says, "Why did you strike Hehaka?"

Wrass mumbles, "I don't like him."

"You want me to hit you?" Ugly waves his war club.

"No."

"Then stop causing me trouble, boy!"

Wrass lowers his gaze and seems to be staring submissively at his moccasins. Ugly turns away to gleefully watch what's happening to the Flint girls, and Wrass whispers, "When I have the chance, he's the first one I'm going to kill. Then I—"

A hoarse roar goes up, and we both spin around. Two of the gamblers have gotten into a fight over the girl by the tree. They circle each other with their knives held low, grinning and calling insults.

"She's mine, Hodigo! You told me I could have her after you were finished!"

"Yes, but I'm not finished, you worthless cur! Wait your turn!"

Hodigo lunges with such swiftness his opponent has no time to evade the blade; it sinks deep in the man's belly. Hodigo whoops in victory and dances back.

Gannajero says, *"Stop it!* No fighting. You know the rules!" She rushes toward them as fast as her old legs will carry her. The feather is clenched in her right hand.

"You stabbed me!" The man wipes at the dark blood that drenches his hide shirt. "Blessed Spirits, you punctured a gut!"

Hodigo laughs, and shouts, "Your heart is next, Cattara!" and charges forward for the kill.

"Guards!" Gannajero shouts.

Kotin tackles Hodigo and wrestles him to the ground, growling in fury. "Stimon? Grab his legs!" Another warrior rushes over and throws his body over Hodigo's flailing legs, holding them.

Hodigo's wounded opponent sits down hard in the frozen grass. His friends gather around him, speculating on his wound. They keep giving Hodigo murderous glances.

"This is just beginning," Wrass whispers. "Look at that blood. He's going to die for sure, and his friends will have to avenge his death."

I say, "Good. So long as they leave us alone, I—"

Gannajero throws her head back and lets out a bloodcurdling shriek that silences every person in camp. She spreads her arms like a huge bird and hops around in a bizarre dance that resembles a Crow hunting mice in a field. As she dances closer to Hodigo and Kotin, men scatter, shoving each other backward to get away.

She stops beside Hodigo with her arms still out. Her black eyes shine and flicker as she cocks her head, looking at him first through one eye, then the other, like a curious bird. Then, with agonizing slowness, she lowers the black feather in her hand toward Hodigo.

Hodigo goes pale when Gannajero leans over him. "What are you going to do with that, old woman?" he shouts, and tries to fight his way free. "Get away from me!"

In an eerie singsong voice, Gannajero chants, "You broke the rules. Hodigo broke the rules."

"You crazy old witch! Let me go!"

She jerks Hodigo's shirt away from his chest and uses the shiny black feather to paint a series of interweaving lines on his flesh. "Hodigo, Hodigo, empty soul, wants the girl, can't let go."

When Hodigo laughs, Gannajero uses the quill to stab a hole in his chest. He lets out a sharp cry of surprise. Blood wells. Gannajero dips the quill in the blood and continues drawing designs while she sings softly. The men standing around seem fascinated. They must be very afraid of her, or else they would jump her, grab their friend, and leave. Instead, they mutter ominously to each other and watch with huge dark eyes.

Gannajero removes a small black bag from her belt pouch. As she tugs open the laces, she says, "You're safe now," and sprinkles a white powder over the bloody designs, then drags out what looks like a freshly dug root. "Open his mouth."

Kotin cranks open Hodigo's jaws, and Gannajero shoves the root so far down his throat that he has no choice but to swallow it.

Hodigo's face contorts, and he spits in Gannajero's face and chuckles, "You can't scare me! I am Hodigo, the greatest warrior among the Mountain People!"

Gannajero smiles as she wipes off his spittle on her cape.

Within moments, Hodigo starts to pant and writhe. Finally he screams as though being eaten alive by wolves. All of his friends back away.

When Gannajero tucks the bag into her belt pouch and rises, Hodigo lets out one last bellow and goes limp.

"There, there," she gently says. "No more bad dreams."

She grins at his friends and walks away. None of them try to stop her.

Holding the bloody feather to her breast as though she cherishes it, she walks out into the meadow to stare up at the sky. The afternoon is shading toward evening. Long shadows fill the forest. She pets the feather while she whispers to herself, or perhaps to the feather.

Kotin releases Hodigo and calls, "All right, get up, Hodigo." He pauses. "I said, get up, you worthless…"

The man doesn't move. Wrass and I stand up to see better. Our guards do not seem to care. They are all breathlessly watching Hodigo.

"What's happening?" I ask Wrass, who is taller than me.

He shakes his head. "I don't know. He's just lying there."

Hodigo's friends bravely move in closer. One man crouches and places a hand on Hodigo's throat. "Blessed Spirits," he says softly. "He has no heartbeat. Is he breathing?" He quickly places his ear over the bloody designs on Hodigo's chest and listens. "I don't…I don't believe it! He's *dead.*"

Gannajero chuckles, and my legs go weak.

Tutelo looks from Wrass, to the guards, and back to me, and sobs, "Odion? What happened to that man?"

I cannot look at her.

The other girl in our group silently rolls to her back. I do not even know her name. She is the quiet one. The child no one seems to notice. Short and skinny, with irregularly cut mourning-hair, she has a face like a chipmunk's: round, with small dark eyes, and two front teeth that stick out slightly. She hasn't spoken a word to anyone…until now. "Don't be s-scared. It wasn't the feather," she stutters. "Sh-she probably used helleb-bore. If you gather the roots this time of year, it—it's deadly."

We all turn to look at her. The attention seems to unnerve Chipmunk. She curls onto her side again and turns her back to us. She's shaking all over.

As I am. My legs feel like boiled grass stems. I sink to the ground and put my arm around my little sister. She hugs me tightly.

"It's all right, Odion," Tutelo whispers. "Mother and Father are coming. They're coming."

7

The northern sentry cried, "Two people on the northeastern trail!"

Sindak climbed to a higher branch in the maple tree where he stood guard over the western trails. Glorious swaths of orange, red, and yellow leaves dappled the mountains. He scanned the winding stretches of trail he could see—even in the soft lavender gleam of dusk, they seemed to glow. But he saw no travelers. Not that it mattered. He would know who they were soon enough.

He sighed and leaned against the massive tree trunk. A tall, muscular young man, he had seen nineteen summers. His beaked nose protruded far beyond his deeply sunken brown eyes. Shoulder-length black hair blew around his lean face. Few women found him attractive, which was one of the reasons his wife, Puksu, had recently divorced him.

There were other reasons, of course, not the least being that she despised him. He had committed two crimes in her eyes: He hadn't yet gained acclaim as a warrior, and they'd been married for two summers without a child. Gratefully, he no longer had to listen to her endless complaining.

His gaze drifted back to the broad plaza of Atotarho Village. Arranged in a rough oval around the plaza were four longhouses, four smaller clan houses, and a prisoner's' house. The magnificent longhouses—the biggest ever built in the history of their people—were constructed of pole frames and covered with elm bark. The Wolf Clan longhouse was amazing; it stretched over eight hundred hand-lengths long and forty wide. The others were shorter, two or three hundred hands long, but still stunning, especially when viewed from Sindak's height. The arched roofs were almost level with his position, soaring over fifty hands high. Each clan was headed by a matron, and each longhouse was inhabited by the male and female descendants of one woman—around whom many legends revolved—and her maternal female descendants. When a man married, he moved to his wife's longhouse.

Since the People of the Hills traced descent through the females, a child belonged to his mother's clan and owed obedience to its clan elders. Women also owned the fields and houses. That's why women decided when to go to war. Everything at risk belonged to them. Men owned little more than their own clothing and weapons. It meant that men had fewer responsibilities, which freed them to fight, hunt...

A shouted curse rang out.

Sindak squinted at the council meeting where over five hundred people had gathered. The village matrons sat in a broad circle around the chief, discussing what should be done next. Chief Atotarho had just returned from a Trading voyage where his party had been attacked. During the fighting, his ten-summers-old daughter had been taken prisoner. War Chief Nesi had tried to track the enemy warriors, but had lost their trail in the rain. Atotarho had been hoping to trade freshwater pearls for food—but had failed.

Everyone was hungry.

The matrons said that the past one hundred summers had been unusually cold and dry. Sindak knew only that the corn, beans, squash, and sunflowers rarely matured. He gazed down at the six women pounding corn in the plaza. They used a hollowed-out log as a mortar, threw in handfuls of dried corn, then beat it to a fine powder with a heavy wooden pestle, about twelve hands long. The rhythmic *thunk-thunk* echoed. A short distance away, two women stood roasting the corn that would be ground in the mortars. They roasted whole ears over an open trench filled with glowing coals. Y-shaped sticks stood at either end of the trench; then ears were hung from a pole placed in the crotches of the sticks and roasted until completely parched, whereupon the women shelled the kernels into a bark barrel and stored it until needed in the mortars. This time of year, there should be two hundred women pounding and roasting corn—not six.

The harvest had been very poor. Meager harvests made people hunt harder, but after so many summers, the animals were mostly hunted out. The simple truth was that they were all growing desperate. Winter was almost upon them, and they had little food to stave off the cold. When people couldn't feed their children, they had to take what they needed from nearby villages. Stealing had become a way of life. When it failed, warfare broke out. Battles had been raging, off and on, for more than one hundred summers, but it had gotten particularly violent in the past twenty summers. That's why a forty-hand-tall palisade of upright logs enclosed the village.

Sindak watched the people milling around inside the palisade. During the autumn, most people spent every moment until total darkness down along rivers where the fields were, collecting the last green-corn cobs or picking late squash blossoms—but everyone knew this council meeting was critical.

Sindak climbed to a higher branch, where he could see better. Two of the clan matrons—both white-haired and skinny—waved their arms. Chief Atotarho, who had seen fifty-two summers, sat with his head down and his eyes closed, as though he could bear no more of this. He'd braided rattlesnake skins into his gray-streaked black hair, then coiled it into a bun at the base of his head and secured it with a tortoiseshell comb. The style gave his narrow face a starved look. On this cool day, he wore a smoked deer-hide cape over his shoulders. Red paintings covered the golden hide, mostly images of men in battle, for he had once, a long time ago, been a great warrior. But now, the cape covered a crooked and misshapen body. Every summer, he seemed to grow thinner. The village Healers said he had the joint stiffening disease. His enemies, however, said Atotarho was a powerful sorcerer, a witch, and his evil deeds had come back to haunt him.

As evening settled over the land in a smoky veil, long purple shadows spread through the forest, filling in the hollows of Atotarho's gaunt face. He had lost his only son in a raid seven summers ago; now his daughter was gone—probably being held hostage, maybe being tortured or worse. Atotarho must be frantic to get his daughter back.

Old Tila—matron of the Wolf Clan—leaped to

her feet and shook her fist at Atotarho. More shouts rang out.

Sindak would love to be down there listening to the arguments, but his duty today was to keep watch on the western trails. Three other guards watched the northern, southern, and eastern trails. The boredom was excruciating. He often caught himself wishing Standing Stone warriors would attack just for the relief it would offer.

Kelek—matron of the Bear Clan—shouted at Atotarho, and the chief dropped his face into his hands as though totally defeated. His False Face pendant fell from his cape and swung in the dim light.

It was strange to see it around the neck of a man. Ordinarily, the sacred pendant was passed from clan matron to clan matron, but Atotarho's only sister had died as a child. Since his mother had no daughter to give it to, the clan had bestowed it upon Atotarho when he became chief.

Sindak stared at it in awe. The pendant was ancient and chronicled the most sacred story of all: the great battle between human beings and Horned Serpent. At the dawn of creation, Horned Serpent had crawled out of Skanodario Lake and attacked the People. His poisonous breath, like a black cloud, swept over the land, killing almost everyone.

In terror, the People had cried out to the Great

Spirit, and he sent Thunder to help them. A vicious battle ensued, and Thunder threw the greatest lightning bolt ever seen. The flash was so bright many of the People were instantly blinded. Then the concussion struck. The mountains shook, and the stars broke loose from the skies. As they came hurtling down, they hissed right over the People. Thousands slammed into Great Grandmother Earth. The ferocious blasts and scorching heat caused raging forest fires. The biggest star fell right into the lake on top of Horned Serpent. There was a massive explosion of steam and—as Horned Serpent thrashed his enormous tail in pain—gigantic waves coursed down the river valleys and surged over the hills in a series of colossal floods that drowned most of the People. Of the entire tribe, only five families remained—the five families who would become the Peoples that today live south of Skanodario Lake.

Sindak propped his hand on his belted war club and checked the western trails again, ensuring they were still empty. He looked toward Forks River, where a group of young women were bathing. Several splashed around in the water. Another group sat on the darkening shore, naked, combing each other's hair while they dressed.

He smiled, letting erotic thoughts run through his mind. He...

"Are you watching the trails, or a woman?" a voice called from below.

Sindak looked down. His friend, Towa, stood below with another warrior named Pova. At twenty, Towa had waist-length black hair and a face women swooned over: oval, with a straight nose, perfect smile, and serious eyes. Unfortunately, Towa didn't see very well, which meant he couldn't hit a longhouse with an arrow at ten paces. But he was especially skilled at war strategy, which was probably why they were best friends. They balanced each other's weaknesses. Towa had recently been wounded in battle and still wore his left arm in a sling.

"I must be watching the trails. We haven't been attacked, have we?" he called back.

"No, but it's only a matter of time. The matrons voted."

"We're going to war to get the chief's daughter back?"

"We are. Our elders do not believe we have the luxury of doing nothing. They say we must act quickly or the Standing Stone People will view our lack of response as a sign of weakness and attack us. That's why I'm here. War Chief Nesi wants to see you. Pova will take your place as western sentry."

"And do a better job," Pova added.

Sindak grinned and scrambled down the tree, using the branches like a ladder. When he leaped off the last branch and landed in front of Towa, a burst of autumn leaves puffed up.

Pova chuckled at Sindak and climbed up to take the sentry position.

"Have I been chosen for the war party?"

Towa said, "You have."

"What about you?"

He yanked a thumb toward his wound and looked miserable. "Nesi told me I can't fight until the wind stops whistling through the hole in my shoulder."

"Well, don't worry. I'll kill two Standing Stone warriors in your honor."

Towa gave him an askance look. "Without me along to watch your back, I fear you may not even make it past our border. Be careful and don't think too much. It always ruins your aim."

"Thinking is for old women. I'll take a good fight over a peace council any day."

Towa walked beside him as Sindak headed back toward the plaza along the leaf-strewn trail. Fragrant autumn winds gusted through the trees, swirling leaves like tiny tornadoes. One careened along the trail in front of them.

"This war party is foolish, Sindak. If you can get out of it, do it."

"Why? I need all the chances to prove the valor I can get. No one is ever going to marry me again if my reputation as a warrior doesn't improve."

"Maybe. But you and I both know that Atotarho's daughter is probably dead, which means many of our warriors are about to die for no reason. Including you."

"But the Standing Stone elders would be idiots to kill Zateri. They could demand a huge ransom of corn for her and get it."

Towa gave him a somber look. "That would make things worse. If we emptied our food storehouses to buy Zateri back, we'd just have to raid someone else to replenish them. Besides, there's nothing the Standing Stone People need. Their harvests were good this year. That's the problem. Their storehouses are overflowing with food, and everyone wants it." Towa exhaled hard.

Sindak shrugged. "We need it. Our people are hungry."

"Yes, I know. We also need their hunting grounds, fishing lakes, nut forests, and especially their agricultural fields. As our numbers grow each year, our harvests get worse. To survive, we must take what they have. Where does it end? With all of us dead?"

Sindak frowned and kicked his way through a particularly high pile of leaves that blocked the trail. He didn't like thinking. Towa was the thinker. Fortunately for the Hills People, they had the greatest number of warriors in the land. They could take what they wanted, and did. No one liked warfare, but if it kept the Hills People alive, it was necessary. Throwing away lives on a futile mission, however, seemed folly.

"I have worse news yet," Towa said. "Because the council was divided on this issue, they only authorized Nesi to take twenty warriors on the war party."

"Twenty?" Sindak stopped in the middle of the trail. "That's idiotic."

"I told you. Get out of it if you can."

Sindak could suddenly envision his death, and he didn't like the looks of it. He started walking again. "I can't. I don't want to spend the rest of my life making excuses for why I didn't die with honor."

"You'd rather be in somebody's stomach than look cowardly?"

"Absolutely."

Two little boys ran up the trail. They veered wide around an ancient maple that fluttered crimson leaves down upon them and laughed as they raced by. Towa smiled and turned to watch them as they splashed their way through a pile of leaves. Two summers ago, Towa had lost his children and wife to a fever. He never talked about it, but sometimes Sindak could still see the pain in his eyes. "Blessed Ancestors, I don't—"

A shout rang through the trees: *"Two Standing Stone warriors coming!"*

They looked toward the northern sentry position, but they could just barely see him amid the dark hickory branches.

"The two travelers are Standing Stone warriors?" Towa's bushy black brows lowered. "Are they imbeciles? We'll slaughter them."

Sindak broke into a run. "Maybe they bring news about Zateri?"

By the time they reached the palisade, fifty Hills warriors were already assembled outside the main gate with arrows nocked in their bows. War Chief Nesi stood in front. A square-jawed bear of a man, his black headband held his chopped-off hair in place. Of medium height, he was all muscle. Ridges of white scars covered his face. Rather than a bow, he carried a massive stone-headed war club in his fist.

The two Standing Stone warriors came up the trail with their hands in the air. The woman was a tall, hard-eyed beauty. Her short hair was jagged, cut in mourning, and she had a sun-bronzed oval face with large dark eyes. She wore her red cape oddly tied over her belly.

"Blessed gods," Towa said, "I think that's Koracoo."

"It can't be," Sindak said disdainfully. "She's too smart to do something like this."

The woman called, "We come in peace!"

Sindak frowned at the man. His face, once

handsome, looked much older than his jet-black hair would suggest. Battle walks did that and left telltale signs. Wrinkles etched lines across his forehead and cut deeply at the corners of his eyes.

"I think that's Koracoo's deputy, Gonda."

"Her husband? You may be right. I saw him once, five summers ago on my first raid."

Every eye in the village focused on the Standing Stone warriors. The matrons whispered behind their hands and made the sign against evil to protect them from any Spirits that may have walked the forest trails with the enemy.

Koracoo stopped short. "We must speak with Chief Atotarho."

Nesi stepped into the path in front of her, blocking her way just outside the palisade. "What message do you carry, War Chief Koracoo?"

Conversation burst out across the village. Everyone knew her name. In the past two summers, since she had been elected war chief, she had killed many of their warriors.

Koracoo fearlessly walked up to stare him in the eye. "My words are for the chief's ears."

Towa leaned sideways to whisper, "She's smart. We can't kill her until we know."

Sindak's gaze went over Koracoo. She wore a red cape painted with the image of a blue buffalo. Her full lips were pressed into a tight white line, and her eyes promised death a hundred times over.

She seemed to have something hidden in her tied cape.

Chief Atotarho lifted a hand. "Nesi, it's all right. Bring her to me."

A path opened through the crowd, and Nesi gestured for Koracoo to walk it. As she did, Gonda started to follow her.

Nesi thrust out his club to block Gonda's path. "Just her."

"I am her deputy. I *never* leave her side."

Nesi raised his club as though to strike, and ordered, "You will do as I say, warrior. Or I will club you senseless."

Sindak had to give Gonda credit; he didn't flinch. He stood his ground and growled, "Get out of my way!"

Atotarho called, "Nesi, let them both approach!"

Nesi glowered at Gonda, but stood aside and allowed him to follow his wife.

Sindak whispered, "She's magnificent, isn't she?"

"Hmm?" Towa said absently. He was staring at Gonda. "Who?"

"Koracoo. She's stunning. Though I've heard Nesi say she's timid, and that's why she doesn't go looking for fights to prove her valor. Do you think she's timid?"

Since Koracoo had become war chief, her

village rarely fought, and then only when attacked. That fact had led many Hills warriors to assume she was weak.

Towa replied, "For a timid woman, she's slaughtered a lot of our best warriors. It's far more likely that she picks her battles carefully."

Sindak grunted. Given the choice, he'd rush in with his bow singing and contemplate the repercussions later—an attitude that had gotten him into more than one impossible situation and earned him more than his share of ridicule. "You think much as she does, Towa. Someday, if you ever learn to aim, you may make—"

Koracoo stopped less than two paces from the chief and said, "Chief Atotarho, I have brought a child that needs your help."

Atotarho glanced at her belly. "What child?"

Gonda untied Koracoo's cape while Koracoo kept her hands on the bulge in her war shirt. When she gently reached beneath her war shirt and pulled out the naked baby, astonished cries rose from the spectators. People surged forward to look, pushing Towa and Sindak closer.

Atotarho asked, "Who does the child belong to?"

"We don't know, Chief. We've been tracking the war party that stole our children after the Yellowtail Village attack. Along the way, we found this baby, alive, but not well. Her soul is loose. She needs food and shelter immediately."

"Why should I care? She's not from this village."

"Perhaps not, but she is one of the People of the Hills. The blanket she was wrapped in bore your distinctive spiral designs."

Atotarho's eyes narrowed suspiciously. "Where is the blanket? Let me see it."

"It was soiled. We left it. But I have no cause to lie to you. She is a Hills child. In one of your villages, someone must be desperate to find her."

Koracoo extended her arms, holding out the baby. Several of the women in the crowd looked hard at the child, but none came forward to take it.

Koracoo said, "Chief, once you notify the other Hills villages that the baby is here, I'm sure her grateful family will arrive and shower you with gifts. Even if her parents are dead, her clan will want her back. Will you deny them the right?"

A pretty young woman, perhaps sixteen summers, shoved through the crowd and asked, "What color were the spirals on her blankets?"

"Red and black."

The woman turned to Atotarho. "Chief, those are Hawk Clan designs. I am Hawk Clan. If you will allow it, my family will take her until her family arrives."

Atotarho looked annoyed, but he flicked his

hand at her, and she scurried forward, took the baby from Koracoo's arms, and hurried away toward the Hawk Clan longhouse.

Atotarho stood stiffly. "I understand little of this, War Chief Koracoo. Please tell me more of your story. Yellowtail Village was attacked?"

Koracoo exchanged a look with Gonda before she replied, "We assumed that perhaps some of your warriors were on the raid."

"No. I was on a trading expedition to the Flint lands. I took sixty of our warriors with me and left the rest here to protect the village while we were away. When did this happen?"

"Five days ago."

Atotarho scanned Koracoo's face, then Gonda's, as though he feared trickery. "When did you find the baby?"

"Just this afternoon. We also think we found the trail of the warriors who stole our children, which means we need to resume our search as soon as possible."

"Your children? You mean your own children? Not just Yellowtail children?"

"My son and daughter were among those captured," Koracoo explained.

Sindak leaned over to whisper to Towa, "Zateri was also stolen five days ago. Is there a connection?"

"How could there be?"

Atotarho said, "War Chief Koracoo, do I have your oath that none of your warriors were involved in the attack on my trading party?"

She frowned. "Your trading party was attacked? I know nothing of it. Half of our warriors were killed when we were attacked, and I ordered the other half to guard our village survivors while they cared for the dead and collected their few belongings. I assure you, Yellow-tail Village has sent no war parties into Hills country."

Atotarho's cape flapped in the wind as he considered her words. In a fearful voice, he said, "Were there other children taken?"

"Yes, several. Though I can't say they were all taken by the same war party."

Atotarho shivered suddenly, as though the thin lance of the forest night had pierced his cape. He stepped closer to Koracoo. His misshapen body crackled as he moved, and his face had taken on an almost skeletal appearance. "I pray it is not so...but I fear we may have a common enemy."

"Who?"

He backed away, saying, "I need to discuss this with our matrons before I tell you more." He lifted a hand to Nesi. "War Chief? Take them to the prisoners' house until I know the matrons' wishes."

"No!" Gonda shouted. "We need to get back on the trail immediately."

"Quiet," Koracoo ordered softly.

8

Nesi pointed his war club. "You four: Sindak, Towa, Ober, and Akio, take these warriors to the prisoners' house and set up alternating watches." Nesi looked toward the eastern side of the village, where the prisoners' house nestled against the high palisade wall. On the catwalk near the top, warriors stood guard. Then his gaze scanned the crowd. People had started to grumble. Several had picked up rocks. "And hurry, before anyone takes a notion to avenge his dead relatives."

"Yes, War Chief." Sindak gestured for Koracoo and Gonda to start walking. Gonda gave him a hostile look, but walked.

Sindak let Ober and Towa escort the Standing Stone warriors, while he and Akio brought up the rear.

Villagers coalesced into a small mob and followed them.

"This could be unpleasant," Akio whispered. He had seen just sixteen summers and spent most of his time lounging around his family's longhouse, which was why he was pudgy and perpetually out of breath. "Our village lost many warriors in that battle with the Standing Stone people last moon."

"Last moon's battle was not with Yellowtail Village," Sindak pointed out. "White Dog Village—"

"It won't matter to the families that lost loved ones. For them a Standing Stone warrior is a Standing Stone warrior."

Akio was right. Sindak kept turning around and noticed that Kora-coo, too, was carefully observing the crowd. Her shoulder muscles had gone tight under her red cape.

Akio said, "I wonder where she stowed CorpseEye?"

"Her legendary war club? I had forgotten all about it."

"It must be somewhere close. She wouldn't leave Yellowtail Village without it. It's supposed to have great Spirit Power." His fat, florid face reddened with excitement. "And it's worth a fortune."

"You're a greedy boy, Akio." Actually, it was a good idea. If they could find it and deliver it to

Nesi, he would reward them handsomely. "Tomorrow morning, if they are still captives, I'll help you hunt."

Akio smiled. "I'll be ready. Maybe we should ask Towa to help, too?"

"I don't think so. He doesn't believe in Spirit Power."

"He believes in wealth, doesn't he?" Akio gave him a sideways look. When Sindak didn't respond immediately, Akio added, "And not believing in Spirit Power is dangerous. Someday a Spirit is going to sneak up on him and suck his souls out through his ears."

Sindak shrugged. "It will be interesting to see if he notices."

As they approached the prisoners' house, one old woman shouted, "Standing Stone filth," and threw a rock at Koracoo. It struck her in the shoulder. Koracoo swung around to glare at the woman just as another rock whistled past, thumped off the house, and bounced across the ground.

"Hurry," Towa said. "Let's get them inside."

The prisoners' house stretched forty hands long and twenty wide. The walls were not of bark construction, but sturdy oak planks, reinforced with cross-poles.

Ober pulled back the heavy door—hung on leather hinges—and said, "Quickly, before we have to put down a riot."

Koracoo and Gonda disappeared into the darkness. Ober closed the door and dropped the plank across it to lock it.

A boy picked up another rock and grunted as he hurled it as hard as he could. It cracked against the house. "You killed my brother!" he cried, and broke into tears. "My only brother! I hope you die!"

Ober shouted, "Get out of here! All of you. Go home. You can call insults tomorrow!"

No one paid attention to him.

Several knots of people formed. They stood around grumbling, shouting insults, and casting hateful glances at the prisoners' house. Stones continued to thump the walls.

Towa turned to Sindak. "I think you and I should take first watch."

Sindak nodded, and they took up guard positions on either side of the door.

Ober scanned the remaining people, then walked over to Towa and softly asked, "Can you do this, Towa? You're still injured. What if trouble breaks out?"

Towa smiled. "Don't worry. I'll be all right. I'll shout for help and hold them off until you get here."

Ober stared hard into his eyes, silently judging Towa's strength and ability. "Very well. Akio and I will sleep with the Wolf Clan tonight." He aimed his war club at Tila's longhouse. It was a massive structure, the largest in the village, and as night deepened, it loomed like a huge dark monster. "We'll be no more than twenty paces away if you need us."

"Thank you, my friend."

Ober and Akio walked away. Several members of the crowd cursed them for protecting the prisoners, knowing all the while the men had been ordered to do so.

"Filthy Standing Stone beasts!" an old woman screamed and hurled a pot at the prisoners' house. It shattered against the planks, and sherds cartwheeled across the ground. "I'll kill you myself before you leave here!"

"I'll help her!" A muscular warrior named Tadu shouted, and hurled another stone. It whacked against the house and clattered down among the broken potsherds.

Sindak, about to comment on the situation, turned to Towa...and saw something. A momentary flash of light, like the flare of a hidden lightning bolt. It frosted the wooden roof of the prisoners' house. He blinked.

"What are you looking at?" Towa asked.

"There's a storm coming. I just saw lightning."

"What lightning? There isn't a cloud in the sky."

"How would you know? You have the vision of a mole. It was right there." He pointed.

Beyond the palisade wall, a gigantic maple stood, its scarlet leaves like drops of blood against the bruised evening sky. In that moment, Sindak would have sworn the great tree had eyes. Eyes fixed right on him.

Sindak glanced at the warriors who stood guard on the catwalk. They held their weapons in tight fists, staring out at the coming night as though they sensed it, too. Many had their jaws clenched.

"Don't you feel that, Towa?"

"Feel what?"

"That eerie sensation, as though there's something out there, something not human. And it's waiting to pounce on us."

"Like a bear?"

"No, not like a bear, like one of the Faces of the Forest, or a Stone Giant. Maybe even a Flying Head." A prickle climbed Sindak's spine. Flying Heads were terrifying creatures. They had no bodies, just long trailing hair, and huge bear paws for hands, which they used to capture and eat anything they wished, including humans.

Towa laughed. "Lightning? Flying Heads? You are very inventive, my friend."

Sindak grinned, but he couldn't shake the feeling that something, or someone, was watching him with glistening, inhuman eyes.

9

Sonon perched on a high branch, hidden by the red maple's thick trunk. Less than twenty paces from Atotarho Village, he had a good view.

They'd found the baby he'd covered with leaves.

Moving carefully lest the sentries on the catwalk see him, he folded his arms beneath his cape and hugged himself. Odd. He could not feel the child's afterlife soul moving through the trees around the village. He'd been hoping to see her again. It hurt that he did not, but perhaps that was good. The girl's soul might be staying very close to its body, which would make it easier for a Healer to find it and tie it to the child's flesh again.

Only the faintest whisper of wings broke the silence as an owl sailed over the treetops and, somewhere in the distance, a wolf yipped. Both creatures were out on their nightly hunts, looking forward to finding and killing prey to fill their bellies with warm blood.

Sonon wiped his sweating hands on his cape. Men needed blood as much as wolves. At the edges of appearance and disappearance, there was always blood.

He studied the warriors who walked the palisade catwalk. He could see their heads bobbing along as though disembodied. All around them, the endless eyes of night were opening, but the guards saw only the shadows cast by the soft glow of the evening. The *communion* of the night was lost to them.

Sonon rubbed his eyes. The communion was all he had. The hunter became the hunted. Perceiver the perceived. The endless eyes stared into eternity, and it stared back.

Sonon patiently waited until the darkness grew too deep for the sentries to glimpse him; then he carefully descended the maple, silently dropping from branch to branch. The wet leaves squished when he dropped to the ground.

Grandmother Moon would awaken soon. He needed to get away before she flooded the forest with light. Slipping behind an elm tree, he faded back into the striped forest shadows and melted into the blackness.

10

"Atotarho looked frightened," Gonda said. "And I don't think he's the type that frightens easily. What do you think scared him?"

The odor of mildew pervaded the dark prisoners' house, and insects skittered across the floor, or perhaps they were mice. Gonda couldn't be certain. If he was lucky, they were mice, and one would scurry close enough that he could catch it and twist its head off to ease his hunger.

"Whatever it was, he didn't want his People to overhear him talking about it."

Koracoo sat on the floor with her back against the wall. In the moonlight that penetrated around the door, he could make out the shape of her body. No one but Gonda would realize how desperately worried she was. He could see it in the tension in her shoulders and in the way her jaw was set slightly to the left.

"Was he worried about alarming his warriors?" Gonda asked skeptically.

"My gut tells me he didn't feel he could trust them with the knowledge."

"Perhaps it's just his war chief he doesn't trust. I didn't like him, either."

Wind gusted outside and breathed through the wall behind him, chilling his back. He wrapped his cape more tightly around his shoulders.

Fatigue numbed him, and long ago, he'd learned that sleep was essential to survival. Death walked at every warrior's shoulder, waiting for him to drop his guard so that it could dull his wits and slow his reactions. Less than a blink was enough.

"You have to get some rest," he said.

"I need to think for a time."

Gonda stretched out on his side and closed his eyes. He tried to concentrate on the sensation of breathing, of air rushing in and out of his lungs. It distracted him from thinking about tomorrow. If all went well, they would return to the murder site, pick up the children's trail, and track them down. If all did not go well...

We're prisoners. Why did I agree to come here when our own children are in danger?

He clenched his teeth to hold back the tidal wave of emotion that overwhelmed him. He'd been trying to take each moment as it came, trying not to see ahead. It did no good to imagine what was happening to Odion and Tutelo. The images only sapped his strength, leaving him quivering and useless.

Koracoo must be enduring the same agony, and perhaps with even more intensity than he was.

Gonda opened his eyes. "Tomorrow. We'll pick up the trail, and it will lead us right to them."

Koracoo did not answer. She stared at the square of moonlight that outlined the door. Occasionally, shadows crossed in front of it, and the house momentarily went black.

Gonda added, "They can't be that far ahead of us. The tracks were only one day old, and it looked like the warriors were herding eight or nine children. That many captives slow men down."

Koracoo leaned her head back against the wall and looked at the roof. Tiny points of light sparkled. Holes. If it rained, by morning, they would be drenched.

"Koracoo, what will we do if Atotarho does not release us in the morning? Have you considered that? It would be a great boon for him to capture War Chief Koracoo and her deputy." He paused, watching her. "We *must* get back on the children's trail as soon as possible."

He waited.

Her silence was like an enormous black bubble

swelling in Gonda's chest, cutting off his air. It was an accusation: *This is all your fault. The destruction of our village. The loss of our children. The deaths of hundreds.*

He tried to calm himself by taking deep, even breaths.

"Please, Koracoo," he begged. "Talk to me. I can't bear your silence."

She exhaled softly and turned to look at him. Her eyes reflected the moonlight like perfectly still ponds. "Gonda, I will talk strategy with you. You are my deputy. But I will not discuss our children. If I do, you will *not* feel better. Do you understand?"

He jerked a nod. "Then let's talk strategy. If they do not release us tomorrow, I've been thinking we may be able to gather more warriors to help us. Atotarho said there are many people who have lost children. If we can recruit a large-enough force—"

"More warriors mean arguments, politics, and intrigue. You and I are enough."

Koracoo shifted her back against the wall and laced her hands over one drawn-up knee. Her short, moonlit hair shimmered with her movements. "Besides, Atotarho is going to release us. He must."

"What makes you think that?"

"Something in his voice. He wants us out there

on the trail. I do not know why, but it's important to him."

"His daughter?"

She took a breath and let it out. "He may think she is with the others."

She had carefully avoided saying, *with our children.*

Gonda proceeded cautiously. "What would make him think that? They were all taken at different times by different warriors."

"Hope often draws connections where there are none. Perhaps he—"

The hissing of warriors' voices silenced her. Her gaze riveted on the door.

Outside, a warrior said, "He's coming this way."

"No, he's not. He's just out for a walk. Probably worried about his daughter."

"He is so coming here! Why would he—"

The warriors hushed. Feet shuffled, and shadows passed back and forth, blotting out the silver gleam that rimmed the door.

"Open the door," Chief Atotarho ordered.

"Yes, my chief."

Wood clattered as the locking plank was lifted and the door swung open.

Gonda studied the five men standing outside. Atotarho carried a small oil lamp. Behind him, moonlight streamed across the village, turning the longhouses into enormous black walls. A few dogs trotted through the night, their tails wagging. Ordinary village sounds echoed: people snoring, children crying, a few coughs.

Koracoo softly said, "Chief? How may we assist you?"

Atotarho moved painfully, rocking and swaying as he entered the house with his lamp. To the warriors, he said, "Close the door behind me."

"But...my chief, you can't go in alone. There are two of them. What if they attack you?"

"I will risk it. Close the door."

The warriors hissed to each other, but obeyed.

As the door swung closed, the lamplight seemed to grow brighter, reflecting from the plank walls like gigantic amber wings. Atotarho wore a beautiful black ritual cape covered with circlets of bone cut from human skulls. When the lamplight touched them, they flashed. A halo of gray-streaked black hair braided with rattlesnake skins encircled his bony face. "War Chief Koracoo, Deputy Gonda, I must speak with you in confidence. Is that possible between us?"

Their people had been at war for decades. It was a fair question.

Koracoo rose to her feet. "You have my oath, Chief. Whatever we say here remains between us."

Gonda got to his feet and stood beside her. "You have my oath, as well."

Atotarho came forward with great difficulty. "Forgive me; I cannot stand for long. I need to sit down." He lowered himself to sit upon the cold dirt floor and placed his oil lamp in front of him. "Please, join me." He gestured to the floor, and Gonda noticed that his fingertips were tattooed with snake eyes, and he wore bracelets of human finger bones. "This will not be an easy conversation for any of us."

Gonda and Koracoo sat down.

Koracoo asked, "What is it you wish to discuss?"

He didn't seem to hear. His gaze was locked on the lamp. The fragrance of walnut oil perfumed the air. Finally, he whispered, "Stories have been traveling the trails for several moons, but only I believed them. She has been gone for many summers—perhaps as long as twenty, though no one can be sure. She's very cunning."

Koracoo seemed to stop breathing. "Who?"

Atotarho bowed his head. "Have you heard the name Gannajero?"

Gonda felt like the earth had been kicked out from under him. More legend than human, hideous stories swirled about Gannajero. She was a Trader who specialized in child slaves. Evil incarnate. A beast in the form of an old woman.

Koracoo softly answered, "Yes. I've heard of her."

Atotarho continued. "Rumors say that she has returned to our country. Many villages are missing children. I have been...so afraid..." He rubbed a hand over his face.

"That your daughter was with her?"

He seemed to be trying to control his voice. "Yes. All day, every day, I pray to the gods to let my Zateri die if she is with Gannajero. I would prefer it. Anything would be b-better..."

Koracoo gave him a few moments to continue. When it was clear he could not, she said, "I understand."

Atotarho's mouth trembled. "No, I do not think you do. You are too young. When she was last here, you were not even a woman yet, were you?"

"I had seen only seven summers, but I recall hearing my family whisper about Gannajero, and it was with great dread."

Atotarho extended his hands to the lamp as if to warm them. His misshapen knuckles resembled knotted twigs. "When I had seen five summers, my older brother and sister were captured in a raid. My sister was killed, but my brother was sold to an old man among the Flint People. I heard many summers later that my brother was utterly mad. His nightmares used to wake the entire village. Sometimes he screamed all night long. He eventually killed the old man, slit his throat, and ran away into the forest. No one ever saw him again."

"Our people, also, have lost many children in such raids."

Gonda looked from Atotarho to Koracoo, watching their expressions. Neither trusted the other, and Gonda wondered what Atotarho might be telling them if they did.

Gonda asked, "What makes you think Gannajero is behind these recent kidnappings? They could be ordinary raids for women and children. In that case, the children are all well and being adopted into families as we speak."

"I pray that is so, but if Gannajero is behind these kidnappings, our children are not well." The chief's eyes narrowed against some inner pain. "My daughter was studying to become a Healer. She knows Spirit plants and how to make poultices. I pray it is enough to allow her to survive Gannajero's torments."

In a deadly earnest voice, Koracoo said, "If Gannajero harms any of our children, I *will* find her. I promise you that."

"Perhaps, but many have tried before you. No one has ever been able to track her. Her trail just seems to disappear. It is said that she has many *hanehwa* at her command, and they help her mislead her pursuers."

Hanehwa were human skins that had been flayed whole by a witch and served as guards.

These skin beings never slept. They warned witches of a pursuer by giving three shouts.

Atotarho opened his mouth to continue, then hesitated.

"Go on."

He looked at Koracoo with shining eyes. "The men she travels with are evil, mostly outcast warriors who enjoy getting rich off the suffering of children. If the children are lucky, they do not live long. Two or three moons, perhaps."

It took all of Gonda's strength to keep his thoughts from straying to Odion and Tutelo.

The lamp flickered when Gonda abruptly leaned forward. "Let's talk about how she accomplishes all this. How do men know where to meet her? To bring her the children?"

Atotarho shook his head. "No one is sure. The last time she was in our country, we thought we understood how she worked. She usually arrived moons before she actually began buying children. The time allowed her to set up her contacts, prepare her trails and meeting places, and assemble her men. She—"

"Then..." Gonda's belly knotted. "She may not have just arrived here. She may have been here for moons?"

"It's possible. Though I suspect not. We almost caught her last time. She knows she must use great care."

Trancelike, Koracoo sat perfectly still, but she said, "Please, go on with what you were saying. You said that twenty summers ago, you thought you understood how she worked. How?"

"We kept watch on her meeting places. She hired men to leave children's toys at specific locations. For example, if she would be at that location to purchase children in five days, the hired men left five toys. Each day that passed, one toy would disappear, until the final day when the man cut the last toy in half, indicating that she would be there that day."

Koracoo straightened. It was a subtle movement. Gonda doubted the chief even noticed, but Gonda understood. Koracoo was remembering the clearing where they'd found the baby. The cornhusk doll had been torn in half.

A coincidence. Our children were taken by Mountain People warriors...

"It would help me"—Koracoo's voice was slow and precise—""if you told me everything you know about Gannajero. Who is she? Where is she from? I know only old stories that make her sound more like a Spirit than a human being."

A gust of wind penetrated around the door, and the golden lamplight cast their shadows like leaping animals upon the walls.

Atotarho clasped his hands in his lap. "I don't know much. No one does. They say she was born among the Flint or Hills Peoples. Her grandmother was supposedly a clan elder, a powerful woman. But during a raid when Gannajero was eight, she was stolen and sold into slavery to the Mountain People. Then sold again, and again. She was apparently a violent child. Several times, she was beaten almost to death by her owners."

"And now she does the same thing to other children?" The hatred in Gonda's voice made Atotarho and Koracoo turn. "What sort of men would help her? How does she find them?"

"I wish I knew. Twenty summers ago, we thought they were all outcasts, men who had no families or villages. Then we discovered one of her men among our own. He was my sister's son, Jonil. A man of status and reputation. He'd been sending her information about planned raids, then capturing enemy children and selling them to her."

Gonda clenched his fists. Warfare provided opportunities for greedy men that were not available in times of peace. Since many slaves were taken during attacks, it was easy to siphon off a few and sell them to men who no longer saw them as human. War did that. It turned people into *things*. It gave men an opportunity to vent their rage and hatred in perverted ways that their home villages would never have allowed.

"Why?" Gonda blurted. "Why did he do it?"

Atotarho bowed his head, and the shadows of

his eyelashes darkened his cheeks. "She rewards her servants well. When we searched Jonil's place in the longhouse, we found unbelievable riches—exotic trade goods like obsidian and buffalo wool from the far west. Conch shells from the southern ocean. An entire basket of pounded copper sheets covered with strings of pearls and magnificently etched shell gorgets."

Koracoo sat quietly for a time, thinking, before she said, "That means it will be difficult to buy the children back."

"Virtually impossible. She profits enormously from her captives. With all the stealing and raiding going on, there are too many evil men with great wealth."

Koracoo toyed with the hem of her cape, smoothing it between her fingers. Gonda frowned. Had she been hoping they could simply buy the children back and be on their way? Where had she planned to get the wealth? They were carrying almost nothing with them—just their capes, canteens, small belt pouches, and a few weapons.

"But..." Atotarho broke the silence. "If my daughter is being held captive with your children, I will give you whatever I have to get all of them back."

Koracoo held his gaze, judging the truthfulness of his words. Atotarho looked her straight in the eyes without blinking. Finally, Koracoo asked,

"Why would you buy our children? We are your enemies."

"If you are willing to risk your lives to save my daughter, you are not my enemy."

Gonda sat stunned. The night had gone utterly quiet. The guards must be holding their breaths, listening. Very softly, Koracoo asked, "Why haven't you already mounted a search party and sent them out with this same offer? Surely you can trust your own handpicked warriors more than you can us."

Atotarho looked over his shoulder, glanced at the door behind him, and whispered, "No. The attack on my trading party was well organized, and they went straight for my beautiful daughter." His knobby hand clenched to a fist. "As there was many summers ago, I fear there is a traitor here. So, you see, I would rather trust an enemy who shares my interests...than a friend who may not."

Koracoo's gaze roamed the firelit shadows for thirty heartbeats—long enough that Atotarho began to fidget. When she looked back, she said, "Tell me more about your trading mission. It's autumn. Many villages have had poor harvests. Raiders are on every trail, Chief, stealing what they can. Especially stealing women and children to replace the family members they've lost. Why would you risk going out at such a time? What were you trading for?"

His long face slackened, making his eyes seem larger. "Ocean pearls and salted seafood. Why?"

"Just curious," Koracoo answered calmly, then added, "We will need to discuss your offer."

"I understand." The chief groaned as he rose to his feet, and the circlets of skull that covered his cape flashed. "I'll leave you the lamp; it will provide a little warmth until the oil runs out." The effort of rising seemed to have cost him all of his strength.

He stood panting for a time before he said, "Many of my people believe I am the human False Face prophesied in our legends. The Spirit-Man who will save the world. It has never been an easy title to bear. Especially now when I cannot even save my own daughter." Without making a sound, he turned and started for the door. "Let me know your decision as soon as you've made it, and I—"

"One last thing."

He turned. "Yes?"

"What assurances do we have that you will keep your part of this bargain? Gannajero will not believe me if I tell her you will pay her later."

Atotarho braced his hand against the door to steady himself. "I will send a man with you who can verify my offer. Now sleep for as long as you can. If you choose to accept, the next few days will not be pleasant for you." He pounded on the door. "Guards? I'm ready to leave."

The door opened, and he stepped into the night.

Gonda watched him walk away with his personal guards. The remaining guards whispered to each other, then turned to stare in at Koracoo and Gonda.

Koracoo asked, "How much did you hear, Sindak?"

The shorter man replied, "Not nearly enough, War Chief."

The door swung closed. After the locking plank fell into place, Koracoo said, "I feel the same way."

"As do I," Gonda whispered.

An excited conversation erupted outside.

Sindak hissed, "By the Spirits, I would hate to be the warrior he sends with Koracoo. He'll be asking for a stiletto between the ribs."

"She won't kill him. She can't. He's her lifeline to saving her own children. Besides, that would be the least of my worries."

"What do you mean?"

"I mean, I'd be far more afraid of what Atotarho would do to me if I failed to bring his daughter home safe and sound."

"Oh," Sindak said. "That is terrifying. I've always worried that someday my own people would turn me into a feast."

Gonda looked at Koracoo. She hadn't moved. "Are you all right?"

"As well as I can be after a discussion about Gannajero."

"Forget about her. Our children were captured by Mountain warriors. Not Gannajero. She died long ago." He grunted. "If she ever actually lived."

For a long time, Koracoo stared at the lamp's flame, as though deep in thought; then she stretched out on her side.

Gonda curled up on the other side of the lamp. The faint warmth was a balm on his face.

The warriors continued talking outside.

Sindak asked, "Have you ever heard of Gannajero?"

"She's a myth."

"How do you know? We hadn't even been born the last time she was in this country."

"True. But if she's as bad as Atotarho said, there would be many stories about her evil deeds."

"Maybe there are stories, but we haven't heard her name because our people are forbidden to speak it—as we are forbidden to speak the names of outcasts."

There was a pause, then Sindak said, "Well, one thing is for certain— if she exists, someone needs to kill her."

"Yes, she..." His voice went too low to hear.

A breath of wind penetrated around the door,

fluttering the lamp's flame and filling the house with the scent of mildew.

"Gannajero. The crow," Koracoo whispered.

"What?"

"Gannajero the crow. Black. Black as coal. It was a song we sang as children. My father used to threaten me when I was bad, telling me that he was going to sell me to Gannajero."

Gonda opened one eye to stare at her. "Your father was a stiff-necked old villain. I never liked him."

After a long pause, Koracoo said, "Not many did."

11

As she slid deeper into sleep, the dream swept over Koracoo...

She led her war party up the trail toward Yellowtail Village at a dead run. Ahead, a gaudy orange halo gleamed against the velvet darkness. Veils of snow gusted by. The pines and oaks drooped mournfully beneath the weight, creaking and groaning in the wind. And in the depths of the trees, she saw the silver-silk flash of people moving. Quiet. Deathly quiet. As though they feared being seen.

Heartbeats behind them, enemy warriors filed out of the darkness, clutching bags or bows, smiling as they trotted right for Koracoo's war party.

"Mountain People!" she cried, and her fatigued warriors charged out to meet them. The sounds of

clubs striking flesh, grunts, and shrieks tore the night.

Koracoo leaped upon the closest man...

Her hands jerked. She woke and glimpsed the plank walls of the prisoners' house and smelled the sweet walnut oil in the lamp.

A dream...just a dream.

But when her eyes fell closed again, the fragrance of the oil became the pungent odor of smoke, and blind terror stalked her as she again charged headlong up the trail with her heart beating in her throat. The sound of one man's feet pounded behind her.

"Koracoo! This is foolish!" her deputy, Deru, called. "We should stay with our war party!"

As she rounded a bend in the trail, he caught up with her. He was a big, muscular man with massive shoulders. He gripped his war club in a tight fist.

"Go back, Deru!" she yelled as two Mountain warriors leaped onto the trail in front of her. Koracoo danced in with CorpseEye. She slammed the first man in the face, and spun to catch the second man behind the knees. When he hit the ground, she was on top of him, hammering his brains out. Her warriors flooded around her, shrieking war cries as they charged for home.

And ran straight into a group of enemy warriors herding freshly captured women and children before them. All of the children were crying, and several of the women clutched babies in their arms.

"Those are my children!" a man cried.

Another yelled, "That's my wife!"

The sharp cracking of war clubs filled the night. Women and children scattered. Koracoo waded in with her war club swinging. In the darkness, she couldn't tell the identities of the children who ran past, but she kept searching, searching for her own family. Asleep, dead, or reborn in another body, she would know her children. She knew the way they moved. Even in darkness, she would recognize them, wouldn't she?

A mother with four children rushed down the trail toward her, one little boy gripping the woman's torn dress and sobbing. As the boy ran closer, Koracoo could see his blood-soaked shirt.

Koracoo broke free of the battle and ran hard for the village. Deru was right beside her.

"Gonda must have been overrun."

"Clearly," Deru answered.

How had she so miscalculated the number of warriors he would need to defend the village? She'd missed something. Something critical. He should have been able to hold off a force three times his size.

Gonda, where are you?

Koracoo leaped over a fallen log and sprinted for the rear palisade, her heart jamming against her ribs. Enemy warriors still surrounded the burning village. Twenty or more stood laughing near the front gates. Were they totally unafraid? Was there no one left to fight?

Forgive me, Gonda...

Tears of desperation burned her eyes. She reached the wall—found a charred section that had been mostly burned through—and used CorpseEye to bash a hole in it. Then she hit the ground and slithered through on her belly.

When she got to her feet, the air was so thick with smoke that she could barely see across the plaza, but the vision stunned her. Every longhouse burned, the flames leaping fifty hands into the sky, and the dead scattered the ground. Cries and screams laced the air. Many people wandered the plaza, turning over bodies, obviously searching for loved ones.

"Koracoo!" Deru scrambled through the hole and stood at her shoulder. "This is dangerous. What do you think you can do here? We should at least wait until our war party catches up before we—"

"I must find out what happened." *And find Gonda and my children.*

Koracoo trotted through the smoke. As she veered around a smoldering section of wall, she caught sight of a little boy crouching in the shadows. Five or six summers, his soot-coated face was streaked with tears. He stared up at Koracoo and clenched his jaw.

"Oh. No." Koracoo headed toward him.

"Koracoo, we don't have time. If we're going to do this, we—"

"I can't just leave him here. He's alone and scared."

She hurried to the boy. Blood clotted his cape. The child stared up at her as she stroked his filthy cheek.

"What's your name?"

"Saga." He fell into a coughing fit. Blood coated his hand when he lowered it.

"Are you hurt, Saga?" Koracoo reached for the cape.

"Not so bad," Saga said. He lifted his arms and allowed Koracoo to look beneath at his chest.

Something in her soul cried out. An arrow must have gone straight through his thin body. Every time Saga inhaled, the hole blew bubbles. But the wound was at the very top of his lung. There was a chance...

"Deru, there must be a place where the medicine elders have been treating the wounded. We need to find it."

Deru gave her a disbelieving look. That was the first thing the enemy did—kill the elders—but he said, "Yes, War Chief."

"It's...it's over there." Saga pointed. "Near the Bear Clan longhouse."

"Deru, you lead. I'll carry Saga."

Deru scanned the smoke as Koracoo slipped her arms beneath Saga and gently lifted him. "Saga, I'm going to carry you over to the medicine elders."

Deru stepped out, leading the way with his war club at the ready.

As they walked, Saga stared up at her with glowing eyes. "I know stories about you. My...my mother...tells me stories at night." His breathing grew more labored. Koracoo could feel the rattling in her arms. She walked faster.

"Good stories or bad stories?"

Saga smiled. "Good. They're stories about our village heroes. Mother says..." He started coughing again, and blood gushed from his mouth. When it was over, he gasped for air.

"Hold on, Saga. We're almost there. The elders will Heal you."

"Do you...remember? Remember...that fight where fifty Flint warriors had you trapped...just you and Gonda...and you killed all of them...before you escaped? Where did that happen? I'm too... tired to remember."

Saga looked up at her with such love and admiration that Koracoo's heart ached. There had only been seven warriors, but Saga didn't need to hear that now. "That was over on the shores of Skanodario Lake."

Saga feebly reached out to touch Koracoo's red cape. He caressed it reverently. "Sometimes...when I play with my brother...I pretend I'm you."

"Well, I hope you also pretend you have another couple of thousand warriors. I need them. Especially tonight."

Weakly, Saga whispered, "It's all right. You'll win."

A wave of futility went through her. "Someday, when you grow up, I'm going to make you one of my deputies."

Saga's eyes went wide. "I'll be a good...deputy."

"I know you will."

Deru was moving quickly, hugging the western palisade wall where the smoke was the thickest. After fifty paces, he stopped and said, "There's someone ahead. I think it's Yanesh. The Speaker for the Women."

The Three Old Women, the clan matrons, announced their decisions through their Speaker. Yanesh was tall and thin, with graying black hair. As Koracoo approached, the woman turned. It was indeed Yanesh. She moved through a sea of wounded people. There had to be hundreds, lying in rows, their faces covered with gray ash from the fires.

Koracoo carried the boy over to where Yanesh stood among the wounded.

"Saga?" Yanesh said. "Put him here. Gently!"

Koracoo eased the boy to the hides spread out over the ground and said, "Get well, Saga. I'm counting on you."

Saga just smiled and closed his eyes as though the walk had taken all of his strength.

"Yanesh, what happened?" Koracoo asked.

Yanesh expelled a breath. She had a catlike face, a broad nose, and long lashes. She had seen forty summers pass.

"The enemy attacked with overwhelming force, Koracoo."

While Koracoo talked with Yanesh, Deru stood guard, his intent gaze scanning the smoke.

"But I left you with enough warriors to hold off—"

"Gonda split his forces."

She stared at Yanesh as though the woman was mad. "That's not possible. I ordered him to keep all of his warriors inside the palisade. He would never—"

"He disobeyed you." Yanesh's mouth quivered as she clamped her teeth. "The council told him not to, told him to keep fighting, but he sent half our warriors outside, and as soon as they were gone, we were overrun. We didn't have enough warriors left to defend the village."

Koracoo gripped CorpseEye in a hard fist. She didn't believe it. "Where is Gonda?"

Yanesh shook her head. "No one knows. He led the group of warriors who ran outside. We haven't seen him since. He's probably..."

Yanesh didn't say it, but Koracoo finished the sentence for her. "He's probably dead."

"Yes, and where were you, War Chief? You were supposed to be back by nightfall!" Her voice broke, and she sobbed.

Guilt ravaged Koracoo. "We were attacked, Yanesh. Hie battle was fierce. I lost one-third of my warriors. The rest of us barely got away—"

"Koracoo!" Deru shouted, and leaped forward, swinging his war club as four Mountain warriors appeared out of the firelit smoke and charged them.

"Yanesh, get down!"

Koracoo lunged forward. When CorpseEye collided with the enemy's war club, a stinging wave flashed up her arms...

And woke her.

She stared at the roof over her head, where

shadows danced in the flickering light of the oil lamp.

Gonda rolled over and stared at her. "Are you all right?"

A terrifying brew of rage and despair was running hot in her veins.

"Koracoo?" Gonda whispered.

She fought down the shout that climbed into her throat, said, "Yes," and closed her eyes.

12
ODION

As Grandmother Moon climbs high into the night sky, a ghostly sparkle filters through the trees and coats the autumn leaves with a liquid silver sheen. The yips of wolves carry on the cold breeze sweeping up the trails, and I have the chilling feeling that the night is filled with wandering forest Spirits. Sometimes I see them flitting between the trunks like white scraps of cloth.

"I need more corn brew!" a man shouts. "Come over here, boy."

I peer out at the warriors who perch like vultures on logs around the fire, using their teeth to rip hunks of meat from roasted grouse. The fire's orange gleam reflects from their greasy mouths and hands. Hehaka wanders through the gathering, carrying a gourd filled with a brew made from fermented corn, pouring it into cups. I watch him. He moves as though he's done this many times, and I wonder how long he's been a slave.

I think about the corn brew, and my throat aches. I tasted it once. Our people pound corn kernels to mush, then leave it until it turns sour. Finally, they pour off the liquid to create the bitter brew. I don't know how anyone can drink it. It scorched my throat like fire.

Gannajero crouches on the far side of the circle with a clay cup of tea in her hands. All night long, she has been staring into the fire, or talking quietly with her deputy, Kotin. He smiles a lot, and his yellow broken teeth glint in the firelight.

I roll to my side and find Tutelo wide awake, staring at me.

I smooth her hair with my hand. "You should be asleep, little sister."

Tutelo sucks her lower lip for a while, then says, "Where's Grandfather?"

"Grandfather?" I find it curious that she did not ask for Mother.

"Yes. Where is he?"

"Oh, let me see, he's been dead for four summers. Don't you remember singing his afterlife soul to the Land of the Dead in the Sky World?"

Tutelo seems to be trying to remember. "There were new green leaves on the trees. It must have been spring."

"Yes, that's right."

Tutelo slides closer to me and nuzzles her cheek against my shoulder. "When is he coming home?"

"Who?"

"Grandfather."

Icy wind gusts through the forest and creeps spiderlike through my clothing to taunt my skin. I feel slightly sick to my stomach. I look down at her. Has her afterlife soul left her body?

"He can't come home, Tutelo. Someday we will go and find him in the Land of the Dead, but I hope that will not be for a long time."

"I miss him."

"I miss him, too."

Tutelo's teeth flash as she flops onto her side and props her head on her hand. Her brow is furrowed, concentrating very hard on what I will say next. "Sometimes the dead come back, but if he can't, we should go see him."

"I don't want to go to the Land of the Dead. Not yet."

"Can I go by myself?"

My heart aches. Is she serious? Does she want to die? "But what would I do without you? You are my only sister. I need you." I adjust Tutelo's collar, pulling it up around her throat.

"Did you see that man in the forest a little while ago?"

I frown. Two men guard us, and warriors are

always walking around in the forest, but she seems to mean something else. "What man?"

"I don't know his name. He just stood out there and stared at us. He picked up one of my copper ornaments." She touched the sleeve of her dress. "I keep losing them."

I glance at the place where the tiny ornaments were sewn. Several are gone, probably torn off by the brush. "Was he one of the warriors?"

Tutelo shakes her head. "No. He wasn't a warrior."

"How do you know?"

"He didn't have any weapons."

My gaze roams the clearing while I consider this. Every man in camp carries a weapon. Quivers bristle with arrows, and belts are heavy-laden with knives, clubs, and human arm-bone stilettos. We are at war. No one can risk being without a weapon.

"He's a human False Face."

"Who is?"

"The man. Can you tell me the story again?"

It takes me a few moments to stop thinking about the man in the forest and understand she's moved on to a new topic. Since the Flint girls were hauled out into the forest, Tutelo has been acting strangely. She found a twig on the ground earlier and has refused to let go of it. She has been clutching it all night long, and this has been a night of desperate nightmares for her. She's awakened me several times, crying; then she twists away from me when I try to touch her. I imagine that in her dreams she is running...running with every bit of her strength. But now, suddenly, she is smiling and longing to hear me tell her stories.

"What story?"

"About the human False Face."

"Do you mean the story about the end of the world, or the contest between Hawenniyo, the Master, and Shagodyowehgowah, the Great False Face?"

"Either one."

I take a breath and think about where to begin. The entire story takes too long. "Well...the ending is the most interesting part, so I'll start there. In the Beginning Time, the Master was wandering around, inspecting creation, when he met the Great False Face. The Great False Face was a huge man who lived far west at the edge of the world. The Master and the Great False Face got into an argument about who created and owned the earth. To solve the argument, they decided to have a contest to see who could command the mountains to move. Whoever made the distant mountains come the closest would win. They both sat down with their backs to the mountains. The Great False Face, Shagodyowehgowah, shook his magical turtle shell rattle—" "And the mountains moved," Tutelo filled in. "Yes, but only a finger's width. Then Hawenniyo lifted his hand and called to the mountains in a great roar, and the mountains immediately moved to rest right behind him. The

Great False Face, who was impatient to see how far the mountains had moved, spun around very fast and—"

"Smashed his face into the mountain!" Tutelo smiled.

"That's right. He broke his nose and jaw. That's why the Faces today all have bent noses and crooked mouths."

Tutelo giggles happily and buries her face in the folds of my sleeve.

I pat her back and stare across the clearing. The warriors do not seem to hear us.

"Like the man," Tutelo says. "He has a crooked nose. Maybe we should give him a name, like Shagoniyoh?"

I don't answer for a time. "You think he's a combination of Shagodyowehgowah and Hawenniyo? That would make him very powerful."

"He is very powerful."

Fear moves like a cold wave through me. If she did see something, it might be one of the *hanehwa*. Witches flayed human beings whole and used their skins to serve as guards. *Hanehwa* never slept. They warned witches of a stranger's coming by shouting three times. Cautiously, I ask, "So he had a crooked nose. What else did he look like?"

Tutelo softly hums to herself and kicks one foot. "He was very tall and handsome—except for his crooked nose—and he had a shining face and cape."

"You mean they shone in the moonlight?"

She shrugged as though she didn't know.

"Did the man speak to you?"

Tutelo blinks. "Why? Are you afraid of him?"

"A little."

She holds out her twig, and in a frightened whisper, asks, "Do you want to hold the club?"

She keeps a tight hold on one end of the twig, but hands up the other end for me to grasp. I wrap my fingers around it.

"Thank you, Tutelo."

It's a war club. I should have known. Mother sleeps with her war club across her chest. Every time I wake in the night and see her holding CorpseEye, I know I am safe.

Tutelo's fingers creep up the twig to touch mine. She sighs.

Did she really see a man? I doubt it. How could a stranger have gotten so close without raising an alarm? He must have been one of Gannajero's warriors but…

Odion.

I stiffen. I swear someone whispered my name. I stare around the forest, searching, before I say, "Did you hear that?"

"He's a human False Face." Tutelo's voice is sleepy. She yawns. "If I went to the Land of the Dead, he would stay here with you."

I do not know what to say to this. Our people

have a legend that foretells the coming of a half-man, half-Spirit False Face. It is prophesied that he will don a cape of white clouds and ride the winds of destruction across the land, wiping evil from the face of Great Grandmother Earth. We have to memorize the story by the time we've seen eight summers.

Tutelo makes a strange hiss, like a snake. It startles me. I stare down at her. As Grandmother Moon continues her journey above the branches, a silver slash paints the middle of Tutelo's pretty face, leaving one eye in darkness and the other glowing like a frosty ball of ice.

She hisses again.

"What are you doing?"

Tutelo presses her forehead against my arm. "He told me I must never cry, or they'll kill me." But with tears in her voice, she says, "Do you know that clouds cry in the voice of the rain?"

A curious numbness spreads through me. These are not her words. Where did she hear them? From one of the other children? I haven't seen her speaking with anyone. We are all so frightened, we've spoken very little, and we are never together during the day. Gannajero sends one or two of us off with different warriors; then we meet again at nightfall. I don't even know the names of most of the captives.

"Rain," she says in a hiss.

And I realize, finally, that the hiss is not a snake sound. It's rain falling through the forest.

"Are you a cloud, Tutelo?"

She nods.

I kiss her forehead. She has found a way to cry without being beaten. I wrap my arms around my sister and hold her tightly.

13

Sindak spread his feet and yawned. Grandmother Moon stood straight overhead. Their watch was almost over. Akio and Ober should be coming to replace them soon. He let his gaze drift over the silvered darkness that cloaked Atotarho Village. The warriors on the palisade catwalk resembled slender pillars of moonlight. Twenty paces away, a happy dog trotted through the night with a half-chewed packrat dangling from his jaws.

Towa whispered, "Where are Akio and Ober? They should be here by now."

"Akio is probably sound asleep. You know how he is. All he does is eat and sleep."

"Yes, but Ober takes responsibility seriously. And one of them better get here soon, or I'm going to faint from hunger. Do you realize we haven't had supper?"

"Why didn't you tell me you were hungry? When I knew I was going to be on sentry duty today, I stuffed my belt pouch with food." He untied the laces on his pouch and pulled it open.

Towa leaned sideways to look inside. His waist-length black hair swung out like a dark curtain. "What did you bring?"

Sindak pulled out jerked venison, wild rice cakes—hard enough to cause brain injury if thrown—and a chunk of half-rancid bear fat. He tore off a piece of jerky, worked it into a gummy mass, then used his teeth to rip off a hunk of bear fat.

Towa winced. "I can smell that fat from here. It's gone bad. Don't eat that."

"It just smells bad. It tastes fine."

"You're disgusting."

"My wife used to say that."

"Please, do *not* tell me why."

Sindak knelt, picked up a rock, and smashed the rice cake to bits. He scooped up the crumbs and ate them. Around a mouthful, he said, "If you chew these *up* together, it tastes a little like quality aged pemmican. I discovered that one night on guard duty."

Towa's brows lifted. "You are truly the bravest man I know."

Sindak grinned and handed him a piece of jerky. "Here. Try it. Eat the jerky first."

"No, thanks."

"Then you are not starv—"

Sindak straightened when he saw Akio and Ober emerge from the Wolf Clan longhouse. Ober towered over the pudgy Akio. Both wore knee-length capes and carried war clubs. He could hear them talking softly.

"It's about time," Towa said. "I'm tired."

"How can you even think about sleeping? That story about Gannajero will keep me awake for days. I'm going to go back to my longhouse, wake everyone, and find out what each person knows about her."

"That should make you a hero with your relatives."

"Well, think about this: If Gannajero is bold enough to steal Chief Atotarho's daughter, she is bold enough to steal anyone's."

"I doubt Gannajero knows that Zateri is Atotarho's daughter. She probably doesn't ask who the children are or where they're from."

"Why not? That could be useful information. There could be rewards out for a child's safe return."

"I suspect no reward can rival what she earns from allowing outcasts to mistreat them."

Sindak swallowed and ripped off another chunk of jerky to chew.

Akio and Ober walked up, Akio panting. "Anything interesting happen?" Akio couldn't walk more than twenty paces without panting.

Towa shrugged, and Sindak said, "Have you ever heard the name Gannajero?"

Akio said, "No, who is he?"

"She. She's a Trader who hires men to steal children."

"Sounds like my grandmother." Ober gestured over his shoulder to Kelek's longhouse. "She's always demanding that we bring back more slaves from our raids."

"That's different," Towa insisted. "Everyone takes children as slaves, but we adopt them into our families. Gannajero, apparently, makes money by allowing them to be used abominably by outcasts."

"What? That's impossible! Anyone who would do that—"

"Wait. I think I've heard of her." Ober's face suddenly slackened. "When I was a boy, my grandmother told me a story about an evil woman Trader. She said there was a Trader who stole children's souls and condemned them to wander the forests forever. Could that be Gannajero?"

"I don't know," Towa said. "What's the rest of the story?"

Ober swung his war club up and rested it on

his shoulder. The chert cobble on top shone in the moonlight. "I don't remember much, just that the Trader used a sucking tube—you know, the sort our Healers use to suck evil Spirits from sick people? Anyway, she used a hollow eagle-bone sucking tube to suck out the children's souls; then she sealed them in a pot and hauled them far from their homes before she blew the souls out into the air again."

Sindak shifted his weight to his other foot. "So that the souls could never find their villages or loved ones?"

Ober shuddered with disgust. "I guess so."

"That's inhuman. If a ghost is near its village, it can see its loved ones now and then, eat the dregs left in the cooking pots at night, and maybe even sit around fires with old friends. But if she releases the soul in an unknown territory, it's utterly alone, cast adrift among strangers, perhaps even enemies. That's a fate only truly evil souls deserve."

"Yes, certainly not the souls of innocent children."

Sindak tried to imagine what that would be like. Sometimes, usually after an illness, or a hard knock to the head, the afterlife soul wandered away from the body and couldn't find its way back. Families hired great Healers to go out into the forests, find the lost soul, and bring it back to the body again. If they couldn't, the soul became a homeless wanderer, forever condemned to travel the earth.

Sindak added, "If I ever meet her, I'm going to kill her as fast as I can.

"After what Atotarho said," Towa pointed out, "I don't think that's as easy as it sounds. What makes you think you're smarter than the dozens who have already tried?"

"I'm not smarter. I'm sneakier."

"Thank the Spirits," Akio said. "I was so afraid." He shivered for effect, and Ober chuckled.

Towa said, "This is not a joke, my friends. If Gannajero is behind this, you'd better think twice before crossing her."

"I'm not good at thinking," Sindak responded. "If I have to do it twice, I'll be dead."

Akio and Ober laughed out loud, and they heard stirrings in the prisoners' house. Someone cursed, probably Gonda.

"Shh," Towa said. "War Chief Koracoo and her deputy have to be back on the trail long before dawn."

Ober hooked his thumb toward the house and whispered, "I don't think my clan will allow Atotarho to free them. Two summers ago, she killed my cousin, Roton. CorpseEye bashed his brains out."

Sindak said, "So? You don't look all that brokenhearted."

"Yes, well, he was a worthless worm, but nonetheless, my family has sworn a blood oath against her. I am obligated to kill her."

"Well, don't do it before you get an approval from Chief Atotarho. He might let Koracoo use CorpseEye on your brain." Sindak paused. "Assuming, of course, that she can find it."

Ober's bushy brows drew together over his pug nose. "Does the chief favor her?"

"Maybe. He was here earlier. He spoke with Koracoo for a long time."

"About what?"

Towa answered, "We couldn't hear most of it. Just that our chief fears his daughter is being held by Gannajero, along with the Yellowtail Village children. He has authorized Koracoo to buy his daughter back."

"Really? For how much?"

"He said only that he would be sending a warrior along with Koracoo at dawn, a man who could verify his offer."

Ober's eyes widened. In a worried voice, he asked, "Did he say which warrior?"

"No."

"I hope it isn't me," Akio whispered. "I'm afraid of Koracoo. I'll have to sleep with one eye open, which means I'll never get any rest."

"Another brave friend." Ober jabbed him in the ribs with his war club, and Akio danced sideways.

"Hey! Stop that!"

Sindak said, "Atotarho wouldn't pick Akio. Half the time, he'd be puffing like a wounded elk and stumbling around through the brush, lost. Gannajero would hear him coming from a full day's walk away."

Akio grinned. "Spoken by a legendary warrior destined to wind up with an arrow in the back of his skull. That is, unless someone can finally convince you to turn around and face the enemy."

Ober and Towa roared with laughter, and half the dogs in the village started barking. Two dogs near the Hawk longhouse got into a fight, and a whirlwind of flying fur broke out. The larger dog must have gotten in a good bite, because the smaller one yipped and ran off limping.

Ober said, "Woosh, even the dogs get upset by stories of Sindak's bravery."

Sindak scowled.

Towa said, "All right. Let's get back to the subject. I suspect Koracoo has sworn blood oaths against many, or all, of our families. Any man ordered to accompany her may be getting a death sentence."

"Surely she wouldn't kill the man who could verify the chief's offer?" Ober said.

"Not before he verified it," Sindak replied. "But after? Who knows?"

They stood around staring at each other for

thirty heartbeats, and Sindak enjoyed the dismay he'd conjured. Fortunately, with his reputation as a warrior, he didn't have to worry about any of this.

"Maybe he'll send Nesi. Nesi can take care of himself." Akio swiveled around, and his plump face and buck teeth reminded Sindak of a beaver.

"He can't send Nesi. The war chief needs to stay in the village to protect it. Though he might—"

A loud knocking sounded inside the prisoners' house.

Akio's eyes went wide. He hissed, "They're knocking on the door. What do we do? Are we supposed to talk to them if they call out?"

From inside the longhouse, Gonda answered, "Yes, you idiot. Since we can't sleep, we've been talking about your chief's offer."

Towa walked over to the door. "Have you arrived at a decision?"

Koracoo answered, "We have. Please tell Atotarho that we accept his offer."

Towa nodded somberly. "Very well." He turned. "Akio, deliver this message to our chief: War Chief Koracoo has made her decision, and she accepts his offer."

"Yes, Towa." Akio puffed away across the plaza toward the Wolf Clan longhouse with his chubby belly jiggling.

"Do you think the chief will come down here

after he knows?" Sindak wondered. "Or will he wait until just before dawn?"

"If it were my daughter out there, I'd want the search party on the trail immediately. Or at least before Ober's relatives find out I'm letting Koracoo go."

"So. We wait?"

Towa gave him a skeptical look. "Would you really want to miss this?"

14

Koracoo stood across from where Gonda knelt, warming his hands over the oil lamp. He watched her in the dim light. Her beautiful face and chopped-off hair glowed faintly orange.

"What are you thinking?" he finally asked.

"I was just wondering what I would do in Atotarho's place."

"Well, I can tell you what I'd do. I'd pick a warrior I trusted to deliver my message exactly. This is going to be very delicate. One wrong word could bring disaster."

She folded her arms beneath her red cape, and the hem swayed around her long legs. "The simple solution is to pick someone who fears him."

"You mean a man who is terrified of what Atotarho will do to him if he fails?"

"Of course. Anyone who is afraid of being executed in front of his beloved family will probably do as instructed."

Gonda got to his feet and expelled a breath. "That's why you are war chief. You're pitiless."

Koracoo's expression hardened. "I'm practical. I remember the lessons old Faru taught me."

"Faru, the Healer? What lessons?"

Koracoo hesitated. She toyed with her sleeve, smoothing it. "When I first exited the Women's House, she sat down with me to tell me my duties as a new woman. Her first lesson was about men."

"Really?" The rituals that introduced new women to the world were reserved exclusively for women. It was forbidden for a man to ask anything about them—but since he had the opportunity... "What did she say?"

"Faru told me that if I truly wished to unravel the knot in the hearts of men, I had to live their deaths every waking moment."

Gonda frowned at her. "What does it mean?"

"I'm still working it out. But one thing I know: Every time I look at one of my warriors, I live his death. On the fabric of my souls, I see through his eyes as he's captured, tortured, and killed. It reminds me of my duty to keep him safe."

"But what does that have to do with unraveling the knot in the hearts of men?"

A faint smile turned her lips. "For most men,

the knot is fear. It's what ties their afterlife souls to their bodies; it keeps them alive. Keeps them sane. If you grasp what a man is afraid of, you can either kill him, or save his life."

He thought back to their earlier discussion. No wonder she would choose a man who feared her. If that's what tied his soul to his body, he would follow her orders exactly and come home alive.

A gust of wind penetrated the house, and the lamp's flame wavered, throwing multiple shadows across the walls and ceiling.

Gonda stared at her. From the first instant he'd fallen in love with her, he'd been doing the reverse: He'd been *dying her life*. She had endured so much, lost so many loved ones, and suffered greatly while serving as war chief. For the past thirteen summers, every shimmer of tears in her eyes had been a little death for him.

He said, "What are you afraid of, Koracoo?"

She cocked her head as though she couldn't believe he had asked. "You know my fears."

"A few of them, yes, but I don't know the fear that ties your soul to your body."

"How is that possible? You have lived with me for thirteen summers, been on war walks with me when we were in danger ever moment, fought beside me when our village was attacked."

Gonda opened her mouth to respond, but hushed voices erupted outside.

Chief Atotarho's voice ordered, "Open the door, Sindak."

The locking plank thudded as it was lifted, and the door swung open. Grandmother Moon's gleam was so bright Gonda had to squint against it.

Atotarho stepped inside. The circlets of human skull on his black cape shimmered. He appeared wide awake. Perhaps he hadn't slept at all since they'd seen him last.

"I understand that you have decided to accept my offer."

Koracoo replied, "Yes, Chief. And we would like to leave as soon as you can arrange it."

The lines around Atotarho's eyes deepened. He nodded. "I will be sending two men with you. It will take them perhaps a half-hand of time to gather their things."

Koracoo dipped her head. "We'll be ready."

Atotarho stepped outside again, and the door swung closed.

The warriors went silent, as though waiting for the chief to speak.

Atotarho said, "Sindak, Towa, you will both be accompanying War Chief Koracoo and Deputy Gonda. Gather whatever you will need. Then I want Towa to meet me at my longhouse as soon as possible."

The chief's steps softly moved away.

After another twenty heartbeats, Sindak hissed, *"Blessed Spirits! Why us?"*

"Oh, stop it. You're not the one he asked to meet him at his longhouse," Towa said. "I wonder what he wants?"

The two other warriors chuckled, and it sounded like men slapping each other on the backs. "Lucky you," someone said. "You have the chance to prove your valor to your chief in a way few men ever have."

"What are you talking about, you imbecile? If we fail, he'll roast us alive and eat us."

"I want your liver," another man said drily.

Sindak replied, "That's not funny, Akio."

Towa said, "Come on. We don't have much time to get ready."

Two men trotted away, and the new guards took up their positions on either side of the door. They continued to chuckle. Akio whispered, *"Gods, I'd hate to be them."*

Koracoo smiled wryly, walked to the wall, and sank down. As she leaned back against it, she closed her eyes, trying to get a few last moments of rest.

Gonda knelt in front of the oil lamp and held his cape open over the flame, letting the heat rise up and warm the inside of the buckskin.

Softly, Koracoo said, "I fear the same thing you do, Gonda—that I will fail to protect my family."

His hands quaked. He lowered his cape and let the warmth seep into his flesh while he squeezed his eyes closed. He tried not to sound like he was strangling when he asked, "Blessed gods, how did you know that was my greatest fear?"

The smiling faces of Odion and Tutelo reared inside him, and he longed to get up and run back to the place where he'd seen the children's moccasin tracks.

Koracoo looked up at him. "The only question that matters now is what does Odion fear? If we know, we may be able to save his life. He—"

"He fears he won't be able to protect Tutelo." Gonda hated to say it. "And he won't. He's not a fighter. We both know that."

Odion feared everything: wolves howling in the distance, unfamiliar sounds in the night. The first time Gonda had taken the boy hunting, Odion had seen six summers. As nightfall descended upon the forests, the boy had started crying, and no matter what Gonda said to comfort him, Odion would not stop. He loved his son with all his heart, but Odion was timid and girlish.

"Fortunately, Wrass is there. That boy is a born warrior."

Koracoo's face tensed. She looked away, and he realized she must have thought his comment was meant as an insult to their son or his upbringing. Because their people traced descent through the female, Koracoo's children belonged to her clan, not his. While a father might be concerned about his children's upbringing, it was none of his business. He was responsible only for bringing up his sister's children.

"Koracoo, I didn't mean to intrude or suggest—"

"No one is born a warrior, Gonda," she said stiffly, and frowned at the flickering oil lamp. "We are made warriors by suffering, anger, and hatred. You fear that your son will never become a warrior. I fear that he will." She squared her shoulders, as though bracing herself for a calamity. "I fear that his training started five days ago."

15

Sindak waited for Towa just outside the Wolf Clan longhouse. He had a bow and a quiver of arrows slung over his left shoulder, and carried a knife, war club, and two deerbone stilettos tied to his belt. Inside his belt pouch, he'd stuffed as much food as he could. And in the pack he wore on his back, he'd placed his cup, a horn spoon, and boiling bag, as well as an antler tine for resharpening stone tools, a blanket woven of twisted lengths of rabbit hide, and an extra pair of moccasins.

He sighed and looked around Atotarho Village. In Grandmother Moon's glow, the frost-coated walls of the longhouses glittered. It was cold tonight, and getting colder. He longed to be on the trail. When a man was walking, he could keep warm. He rubbed his arms beneath his cape and shivered.

From inside the longhouse, he heard Towa say in a low voice, "Yes, my chief." Then, "Yes, I will."

Towa ducked beneath the curtain that covered the longhouse entry and marched toward him. Sindak frowned. Towa's face had a sober, vaguely lost expression.

Towa passed Sindak, said, "Let's go," and continued on toward the prisoners' house.

Sindak trotted to catch up. "What happened in there? It took a long time."

Towa flipped up the hood of his cape. "The chief just wanted to make sure I understood my duties."

"Those are also my duties, so what did he tell you?"

Towa glanced at him. He'd pulled his hair back and braided it. The style made his face look leaner and more dangerous. His unblinking eyes resembled moonlit holes. "We are to find his daughter and bring her back. No matter the cost."

"It would have taken five heartbeats for the chief to tell you that. What else did he say?"

Towa shook his head, indicating that he couldn't repeat a word of it.

"Are you telling me he gave you secret orders?"

Towa looked away.

"But I'm much braver than you and a better

warrior. If anybody was going to be trusted with secrets, it should have been me."

Towa glared at him. "I didn't *ask* for this burden. I'd gladly give it to you if I could."

"Burden? What burden?"

Towa focused his gaze on the prisoners' house, where Akio and Ober stood guard on either side of the door. Both friends were watching them with wide, expectant eyes. As Towa and Sindak came closer, they started whispering to each other.

Akio called, "Is the chief coming?"

"No," Towa answered. "You are to release the Standing Stone warriors and open the palisade gates for us."

Suspiciously, Ober said, "On whose authority? Yours?"

"Yes, mine." Grumbling, Towa jerked a magnificent carved gorget from his shirt and let it swing before their eyes.

"Blessed gods," Ober hissed. "The chief gave you his sacred pendant? That means he grants you his authority. Whatever you say comes as if from the chief's own mouth."

Sindak stared openly at the pendant. Very few people had ever seen it up close. It was not a thing for ordinary eyes. He could feel Power pulsing around the twisted features of the False Face, representing Horned Serpent, and the falling stars that filled the background. It was big enough to cover half of a man's chest. Legend said that at the time of the cataclysm, two pendants had been carved by the breath of Horned Serpent. One belonged to the chief. The other to the human False Face who would don a cape of white clouds and ride the winds of destruction across the face of the world.

Sindak whispered, "Put it away, Towa. Our eyes should not look upon such a powerful thing."

Towa tucked it back into his shirt and gestured to the door. "Open the door to the prisoners' house, Ober. In the meantime, Akio, tell the guards on the catwalk that the chief has ordered the palisade gate to be opened."

"Yes, Towa." Akio waddled up to the palisade gate and shouted, "Bostum? The chief has ordered that the gate be opened so that War Chief Koracoo and her party may leave."

"*What?*" Bostum shouted back. "You're just a fat boy, Akio. I'm not going to listen to you. Where's Nesi? I want to hear it from him."

Akio turned back to Towa, obviously thinking Towa would bring out the pendant again. Instead, Towa said, "Go and fetch Nesi. The fewer people who know about the gorget, the better."

"I'm going." Akio hurried across the plaza and ducked into the Hawk Clan longhouse.

As Ober lifted the locking plank and swung open the door to the prisoners' house, Sindak waited beside Towa. His friend was breathing hard, as though the weight of the pendant resting on his chest was suffocating him.

Sindak whispered, "How's your belly?"

Towa gave him an askance look. "Why would you want to know?"

"Not even a hint of weasels thrashing around in there, trying to get out?"

"Well, small weasels..." He halted when War Chief Koracoo and Deputy Gonda walked out and stood quietly in the brilliant moonlight. Koracoo adjusted her cape, then tied her belt more securely around it.

"Towa. Sindak." She looked both of them straight in the eyes. "Are you ready?"

Towa answered, "Yes, War Chief. You should know that Atotarho has instructed us to obey your orders as we would his."

Gonda's heavy brow wrinkled. He glanced suspiciously at Towa, then Sindak, and finally said, "We'll see how long that lasts."

"What do you mean?"

Gonda grimaced as he walked past, heading toward the palisade gate.

Koracoo looked at Towa. Her chopped-off hair fell in uneven lengths around her beautiful face. "As I understand it, Towa, you are the chief's personal representative. You are carrying his sacred gorget, aren't you?"

"I am." Towa shifted uncomfortably.

Koracoo searched his eyes, and Towa must have felt her scrutiny like a blow to the stomach, for he stopped breathing. "Very well. It's after midnight. Let's get as close to the clearing where we found the baby as we can; then we'll eat and try to rest until we have enough light to track."

Without waiting for a response, she led the way to stand beside Gonda in front of the gate.

"They must want to be out of here badly," Sindak said.

"Wouldn't you? They took their lives in their hands when they brought the baby here."

"They must have thought that baby was very important," Sindak commented. "We should have killed them. They're our enemies."

"Well, keep that to yourself. The chief says that in this one instance, they are our allies and we are to treat them as such."

"Until they prove otherwise, you mean."

Towa tightened the laces on his leggings. "Atotarho told me our first duty is to protect Zateri, then ourselves, and finally the other children."

"He gave no orders about protecting Koracoo or Gonda?"

"They can protect themselves, and he knows it."

Sindak turned when Nesi stalked forward with Akio trotting behind him. In the darkness, Nesi looked like a wounded giant. The scars on his face might have been a tangle of white cords.

He marched straight to Towa, placed his hands on his hips, and barked, "Who gave you the authority to tell the guards to open the gate?"

Towa turned so that Koracoo and Gonda could not see the pendant, and drew it out for Nesi. Nesi's face slackened. For several heartbeats, he seemed confused as to what to do about it. Sindak thought Nesi might even be thinking that Towa had stolen the sacred gorget.

Finally, Nesi said, "Why do you have that?"

"The chief is sending us out on a special mission with War Chief Koracoo to find his daughter and bring her home safely."

Nesi's scars twitched. "Why you two? You're the last two warriors I'd choose."

Sindak shrugged as if he had no idea, but Towa said, "You should, perhaps, ask the chief."

Anger, or maybe suspicion, flared in Nesi's eyes. He looked up and lifted a hand to Bostum. "Open the gate, Bostum. Let them out, then close it up tight."

"Yes, War Chief."

Nesi glanced hatefully at Koracoo and Gonda, gave Sindak and Towa a final unflattering appraisal, and stalked back toward the Hawk Clan longhouse.

Towa put a hand to his heart and sucked in a

fortifying breath. "Blessed Spirits, I thought for a moment he was going to tackle me and rip the gorget from my throat."

"So did I. He seemed very unhappy that we had been chosen for this task."

"Well, he does think we're useless. Maybe he thought the chief would select him. Who knows?"

Sindak pointed to Towa's wounded arm. "I notice that you removed your sling. I assume that's so it's not as obvious that you are useless."

"Exactly."

"You should have left it on. Koracoo and Gonda are going to find out soon enough anyway."

"Thanks. I feel better."

They headed toward the gate. By the time they got there, Bostum had pulled back the locking plank and opened the heavy gate. Koracoo went first, followed by Gonda, Towa, and lastly, Sindak.

Only the faint whisper of frozen leaves underfoot filled the night as they walked out into the dark forest.

They'd gone perhaps fifty paces when Koracoo stopped beside a sassafras tree. Clusters of shriveled blue fruit clung to the tree branches.

"What's she doing?" Sindak asked.

Towa shrugged.

Gracefully, Koracoo knelt, reached behind the tree, and pulled CorpseEye from beneath a bed of leaves. The legendary club glowed in the moonlight.

Sindak stared openly and hissed, "There it is. Blessed gods." He fervently hoped that in the days to come, she would not have an excuse to use it on him.

16

As they marched up the twisting moon-silvered trail, the air was fragrant with the ghosts of long-dead ferns and rushes. Gonda shivered beneath his cape. With each frigid gust of wind, the trees shook moisture down upon them. The drops sprinkled Koracoo's hood and shimmered like white beads upon her shoulders. Black spruces and ankle-deep drifts of moldering leaves lined the mountain path. He slogged his way through them behind Koracoo.

Sindak and Towa brought up the rear. His new allies had been quiet for most of the journey, but had started to whisper to each other. It annoyed Gonda. Even barely adequate warriors knew better. A man on the war trail did not speak. He listened for the sounds of the enemy, or he wound up with his throat slit. Either by his enemies, or his friends.

The trail curved around a hillock of rounded boulders. As he silently passed, in the night sky high above, he heard the distinctive, lonely honks of geese.

Gonda looked up, trying to see them, and made out a faint chevron of black dots, headed south. Their calls were melodic and soothing.

Sindak said, "The medicine elder Old Kelek told me that geese mate for life. Do you believe that, Towa? I mean, they probably don't trace descent through the female, right? If women don't rule the goose world, why would males mate for life?"

"Are you brainless? Shut—"

"Old Kelek also told me that the Flint People build platforms in the marshes for them to nest upon. The geese. Not the Flint People. It makes hunting them much easier. We should do that."

"Hunt the Flint People?" Towa asked.

"No, the geese, you moron. We already hunt the Flint People."

"Silence!" Gonda ordered and glared at them. They stared at him with wide eyes. They made a strange pair. Towa stood a head taller than Sindak and had broad muscular shoulders. Sindak, on the other hand, was lean and homely. His beaked face and deeply sunken eyes reminded Gonda of a winterkilled hawk that had been drying in the sun for too long. But the youth moved like a warrior. He was agile and catlike, whereas Towa always seemed to be stumbling over something. A fine pair of companions for a war walk.

Koracoo veered around a mound of autumn leaves, and Gonda saw the cornhusk doll clearing. Moonglow sheathed the crooked limbs of the gigantic oaks that fringed the meadow, icing them in white.

"At last," Gonda whispered. "Let's eat something and get to sleep."

"I agree. Daylight is not far away."

Gonda trudged into the clearing. He unslung his bow and quiver and set them aside; then he knelt and began scooping aside leaves. Koracoo tied CorpseEye to her belt and crouched to help him.

Sindak and Towa stood looking on as though mystified.

Curtly, Gonda said, "I'll build the fire if someone else will gather wood. Like you two."

Sindak scanned the leaf-filled clearing. "Are we camping here? It looks damp. Why don't we get out of the wet leaves?"

Irritated, Gonda said, "Why don't you close your mouth and go collect wood?"

Sindak stiffened. Gonda's tone had obviously offended the youth, but Gonda didn't care. When Sindak and Towa made no move to obey his order,

Gonda rose to his feet to be even more unpleasant...

Koracoo said, "Sit down, Gonda."

He clenched his fists, gave her a distasteful glance, and then did as she'd instructed.

Koracoo explained, "Sindak, once we get the fire built, it will be warmer sleeping among the leaves than out in the open. If you and Towa will gather some dry branches, we'll cook something to warm our bellies; then we'll rise before dawn. That means we don't have much time to rest."

Sindak muttered something Gonda couldn't hear, but it sounded mutinous. Gonda glowered, and Sindak took a threatening step toward him.

"Enough," Koracoo ordered in a voice that brooked no disagreement.

Towa quickly grabbed Sindak's arm. To Koracoo, he said, "We will gather wood, War Chief."

As he and Sindak wandered away and started collecting wood, Koracoo watched them. They moved through the oaks, breaking the dry lower branches from the trees, casting glances at Koracoo and Gonda. "They're curious, aren't they?" she asked.

"Curious? They're both simpletons. We should send them home before they get us killed."

Koracoo kept her eyes on the young men, studying them. "They are wreckless. At least

Sindak is. I thought for a moment he might try to take you."

"That would have been a fatal error."

"It would also have been your fault. You seem determined to split our party in two. Stop it. We all have to be on the same side."

Anger rose hotly in his veins. In a hushed voice, he said, "They are Hills People, Koracoo. They don't know what *our* side is! They are our enemies. Do you really think they want to help us rescue *our* children?"

Her expression turned to stone. "I am always prepared for the worst, Gonda. But until they demonstrate they are not on our side, I plan to treat them as I would my own warriors."

"Well, that's foolish. They probably have secret orders to kill us and our children as soon as they have Zateri."

"They may, indeed." She tucked a lock of wind-whipped black hair behind her ear. "But given their inexperience as warriors, I doubt they can accomplish it. And our best defense against treachery is to try and befriend them."

"Befriend them? Are you joking?"

"We will be traveling together for many days, Gonda. Perhaps, moons. It will not help us if you are constantly antagonizing them. I won't tolerate it."

He felt like he was about to explode. To ease

some of his tension, Gonda dug into the leaves with a vengeance, scooping armfuls away and piling them to the side. He needed to clear a swath of ground large enough for three people to sleep. One person would always be on guard. Through gritted teeth, he finally said, "I am loyal to you, you know that. I will, of course, follow your orders."

"Thank you."

When he'd scooped enough armfuls away to reveal a broad circle of bare earth, his anger had faded. He sank down and slipped his pack from his shoulders.

Koracoo unslung her pack, as well. While she rummaged around inside, pulling out sacks of jerky, cornmeal, and dried onion, Gonda fought the overwhelming sensation of despair that descended over him like a black fog. His heart was beating a slow, dull rhythm against his ribs.

He removed the small stone pot where he kept coals from the morning fire. "By the way," he said, trying to lighten the darkness, "if these are the two best warriors Atotarho has, we need to attack the Hills People immediately. We should be able to conquer the whole nation in a few days."

She smiled faintly. "I'll consider it. After we've found the children."

Gonda removed the stopper from his pot and dumped the coals on the ground, then began carefully selecting the driest leaves he could find and piling them over the coals.

Koracoo's smile faded, and her gaze returned to Sindak and Towa, who were cracking off dead branches while they murmured to each other. She shook her head lightly. "I can't figure it out, but there's more here than is apparent, Gonda."

"What do you mean?"

"I'm not sure yet. I need to think about it for a time. By morning, I'll have pieced it together better."

Koracoo pulled her boiling bag and tripod from her pack. The tripod, three long sticks tied at the top, stood five hands tall. She spread the tripod's legs, then suspended her boiling bag in the center and tied the laces to the top of the tripod.

"I still have a full water bag," Gonda said. He removed it from his belt and handed it to her.

Koracoo loosened the laces, tipped it up, and poured the water into the boiling bag. "That should make enough soup to feed us tonight and tomorrow morning."

As Koracoo started crumbling venison jerky into the boiling bag, Gonda bent down to blow on the leaf-covered coals. The longer he blew, the brighter the glow became until the scent of smoke rose. It took several moments before the leaves caught and flames flickered. Gonda added more dry leaves to keep the small blaze going.

When Sindak and Towa saw the flames, they trotted across the clearing to dump their armloads of wood beside the fire.

"I could eat an entire deer," Towa said, and crouched before the fire. "What are we having?"

"Jerky and watery cornmeal gruel with dried onions," Koracoo said.

"Good enough." Towa smiled, trying to be pleasant. "While we were out in the trees, I picked up a good cobble for the boiling bag."

He pulled a rounded stone the size of his fist from his pack and set it at the edge of the flames; then, he helpfully began laying twigs over it. As the wood burned, it would heat the rock.

Sindak made no attempt to help. He knelt and glanced uneasily at Gonda and Koracoo. Oddly, that made Gonda feel better. Getting too friendly too fast was the dead giveaway of an assassin.

As the tiny blaze grew to a fire, Koracoo lifted the sack filled with dried onions and poured some into the boiling bag. The sweet fragrance of onions rose.

In anticipation, Towa pulled his wooden cup from his belt pouch and nervously turned it in his hands while he waited.

Sindak's nostrils flared at the aroma. To Towa, he said, "My wife used to make jerky and cornmeal gruel."

Towa looked at him askance. "Puksu cooked?"

"Not often, but occasionally, when she wasn't over at her mother's place in the longhouse cursing me."

"Was it good?"

"Her cursing?"

"The gruel."

"Oh. Sure. Unless she'd poisoned it. I don't think it's healthy for a wife to know so many Spirit plants. The temptation is too strong."

"As I recall, the study of Spirit plants was something she took up after she married you."

Sindak scratched beneath his chin. "She told me she wanted to become a Healer. I thought it was suspicious."

Towa nodded.

Gonda sat quietly for several moments before he said, "I hope you two are a whole lot smarter than you look or sound."

The two youths blinked, and Koracoo glared at Gonda with lethal intent.

"Uh...," Gonda said with a shrug. "That was a joke."

"Oh. Ha." Towa smiled politely.

Sindak looked like he wanted to get his hands around Gonda's throat.

Gonda placed more branches on the flames and glanced around the clearing. Fire shadows danced through the massive oak limbs. He watched them for a while; then his gaze returned to Sindak, and he found the youth staring at Koracoo's breasts as she bent to stir the gruel. The neck of her cape had fallen open, revealing a glimpse of her chest. Generally, the youth had dark, beady eyes that shifted as though rolling around loose in their sockets, but not now. He'd fixed unblinkingly on Koracoo's breasts like a starving wolf about to leap upon an unsuspecting rabbit.

"Sindak," Gonda said.

He turned. "What?"

"Life is an uncertain thing. You might want to consider that."

Sindak's brows lifted. A small smile tugged at the corners of his mouth; then he nodded and looked away. He had understood perfectly, but Koracoo did not. She glanced between Gonda and Sindak with a hostile expression on her face.

Gonda explained, "Nothing to worry about. I'm befriending him." He casually watched the sparks flit upward into the night sky. Only the brightest campfires of the dead shone in the wash of moonlight.

"War Chief?" Towa said. "The cobble is probably hot enough. Should I drop it into the boiling bag?"

"Yes, thank you."

Gonda evaded Koracoo's eyes. She still had her evil gaze squarely on him.

Towa rose, pulled two branches from the

woodpile, and used them to pick up the hot rock. As he walked around the circle, he tripped, almost dropped the rock down Sindak's collar, and continued to the bag. When he dropped the cobble into the water, an explosion of steam gushed up, and the rich scent of venison filled the air.

They sat in silence for another one hundred heartbeats; then Koracoo said, "Gonda, please fill everyone's cup. Starting with mine." She pulled her cup from her pack and handed it to him.

Gonda filled it and handed it back.

"I'm taking first watch." She rose, holding her cup in both hands. "Towa, I'll wake you in two hands of time. You'll take the last watch."

"Yes, War Chief."

Koracoo walked out into the darkness and vanished amid the trees.

As soon as she was gone, desperation returned to taunt Gonda. She should have picked him for the last watch. Gonda wouldn't sleep a wink with Towa on guard. He ordered, "Towa, give me your cup."

Towa handed it over, and Gonda returned it full. When Sindak started to extend his cup, Gonda said, "This is awkward, isn't it? I mean, when I was a child, if anyone had told me I'd be sitting around a war camp joking with two Hills warriors, I'd have kicked him in the groin for being an imbecile. But here I am." He filled Sindak's cup and handed it to him.

Sindak looked down into the gruel as though he suspected Gonda had spat in it. "I'm glad I didn't know you as a child."

"Let's face reality. None of us is going to trust the other for a long time, if ever, so I guess we should just try to make the best of it. What do you say? I agree not to slit your throat in the night, if you agree not to slit mine or Koracoo's."

A gust of wind blew Towa's long black hair around his face. In a slightly confused voice, he said, "Deputy, we are bound by our chief's orders to obey you. We will do whatever you tell us to."

"I take that as a yes. What about you, Sindak?"

Sindak leaned over to sniff his cup, and the nostrils of his beak nose flared. When he looked up at Gonda, suspicion pinched the lines around his eyes. "Are you still married to Koracoo?"

"What?"

"Are you still married? She doesn't act like it, but you do. Are you?"

Gonda sat back. "No, she divorced me. Why? Thinking about crawling between her blankets some night?"

"Of course not."

"That's smart, because you'll have a stiletto through your balls before your voice can change. Think how embarrassing that will be."

Sindak took a drink of his gruel and wiped his mouth on his sleeve. "You *are* trying to befriend me. Thanks for the advice."

Gonda dipped his cup full of soup, swallowed it in eight big gulps, then glared one last time for good measure and rolled up in his blanket to sleep.

After a few hundred heartbeats, Towa whispered, "I don't think he likes us."

17
ODION

The fire has died down to a crimson gleam, leaving the woods frosty and smoke-colored, streaked here and there by the last echoes of moonlight.

I've been shivering for over a finger of time. I watch Gannajero through the weave of frozen grass stems. A pile of riches rests on the ground before her: quivers decorated elaborately with porcupine quills...etched copper breast-plates...a shirt covered with elk ivories...and many necklaces, stone tools, feather pouches. But she is apparently unhappy. She paces before two Flint warriors, shouting and waving her fists. One is a big, crazy-eyed man. He is stocky, and geometric tattoos cover his face. The sides of his head are shaved, leaving a central roach of hair on top. White feathers—war honors—decorate it. Each man holds a Flint girl by the arm. One of the girls weeps inconsolably. The other keeps trying to fight.

"You fools! This isn't enough to buy one of the girls, let alone two! Release them!" Gannajero's wrinkled face has contorted into a hideous long-nosed god mask.

The fighting Flint girl shouts, "Leave my little sister alone! Let her go. Take me! Take me!" and repeatedly lunges at the big crazy-eyed man, who smiles and shoves her to the ground...over and over.

Her sister just hangs in the thin man's grip like a soaked rabbit-fur doll, sobbing.

I don't know where the other Flint girl is...or Hehaka. He's gone, too.

"Give them to me, or the girls stay here!" Gannajero yells.

"I'm not giving you my soul!" the crazy-eyed man shouts back. "You can't have it! I've given you everything else I own!""

"Then you can't have the girls." Gannajero folds her arms over her chest.

Kotin and three other men move in, surrounding Gannajero as though to protect her, or perhaps to kill the men if it becomes necessary. They have war clubs in their fists.

I lift my gaze to the trees. Their faint shadows are like smudges of gray silk in the branches, swaying, flying.

"What's ha-happening, Odion?" Tutelo whispers.

"They're still fighting. Try to sleep."

"I can't sleep!" She weeps softly. "No one could sleep with all the shouting."

I stroke her long hair and hug her. "Then just don't cry. Be a cloud. All right? Remember what Shagoniyoh said. Be a cloud."

Tutelo squeezes her eyes closed and hisses like a snake.

From my right, Wrass murmurs, "The old woman has lost her soul. She's totally insane."

Chipmunk stutters, "M-Maybe she needs one of their souls to p-put in her own body."

"Maybe," I answer. "I just wish she'd kill them and take the girls back. I—"

When Gannajero whirls around and stalks toward us, Wrass yips, *"What—?"*

"Don't move!" Gannajero says. Ten paces away, she spreads her arms like a bird and spins toward us. She is so graceful she might be a crow sailing on wind currents.

We all sit as if carved of wood. There is a rotten blood stench about her. It envelops me as she leans over. Wrass clenches his jaw and stares at her, but I turn away, too afraid to look into her wild black eyes.

A heartbeat later, Wrass lets out an enraged cry, and I jerk around. Gannajero has grabbed his left hand. "Hold him!" she orders our guards.

Ugly and Worm swoop down, pin Wrass to the

ground, and hold him as Gannajero drags a hafted quartzite blade from her belt. It glints.

"I'm going to teach you a fine lesson, boy," she says. "You think that someday you will kill one of my men and escape? Watch carefully."

She slams his hand to the frozen ground and saws off the top of his little finger, neatly severing it at the joint. Wrass kicks and writhes, twisting to get away while he screams.

Gannajero picks up the bloody tip of his finger and cradles it in both hands as though it's a great prize. "Yes, yes, watch now."

The guards release Wrass, who sits up, whimpering, and stanches the flow of the blood with his cape.

"Wrass!" I madly crawl over to him and press my hands atop his, trying to place enough pressure on the wound to congeal the blood.

Wrass seems to be in shock. He can't take his eyes off Gannajero as she slowly, deliberately, bird-walks back across the clearing to where her two men hold the Flint girls.

Crazy-Eyes says, "I am not Hodigo, old woman. That doesn't scare me. I have cut a thousand men apart!"

The wind must have caught the coals just right. They flare suddenly, and firelight coats Gannajero's face like a thick amber resin, catching in a searing line along her extended arm. "You're really not afraid?" she asks mildly.

"Of course not!"

Gannajero steps closer, tempting him to run. He stands his ground and grips the Flint girl's arm tighter. He can't run now. The eyes of every man in camp are upon him.

Gannajero smiles as she walks right up to him, then uses the bloody fingertip to paint a zigzagging Spirit line down his sleeve. He flinches, but does not flee. "Oh, yes, look." She turns to his friends and nods. "He is brave."

He throws out his chest and glances at his partner, who holds the other Flint girl. "See? I told you. She's just an ugly old woman."

Gannajero smiles and reaches into her belt pouch. When she pulls out a hollow eagle-bone-sucking tube, the man goes rigid. He starts to back away, dragging the girl with him.

Before he can get too far, she orders, "Stop."

As though the order enrages him, he stops and whirls around to face the old woman. The Flint girl fights harder—she's kicking his legs and butting her head into his side—but he barely seems to notice. He stares at the sucking tube and laughs. As Gannajero walks closer, he says, "Don't be foolish, old hag. I'll kill you."

She stops and cocks her head back and forth in that eerie birdlike manner. "Let's bargain. If you let you suck out your afterlife soul, I'll let you have the girl and return your magnificent copper breastplate."

The man grins and extends his arm. "All right, but hurry. I have plans."

Gannajero slowly tiptoes forward, rubs the fingertip over the tube, consecrating it, then places the tube against his exposed wrist and sucks. Then she suddenly leaps backward.

His friend says, "Dinyoteh? Are you all right?"

"Of course, I—I am."

"Did it hurt?"

"Don't be foolish. I don't feel any different at all. If she thinks she has my soul, that's fine. I know she doesn't. Let her suck yours out, too, so we can go."

His friend pales. "I don't—"

"I'm telling you, Sondakwa, it's all nonsense. Do you really think this ugly old woman can steal souls?"

His friend hesitantly extends his arm, and Gannajero edges forward, places her tube against his flesh, and sucks out his soul.

When she's finished, she pulls a small pot from her belt pouch, removes the wooden stopper, and blows their souls into it. Then she tucks Wrass' fingertip into the pot and stuffs the stopper back in. "All right," she says with a flick of her hand. "Take the breastplate and the girls."

Crazy Eyes, Dinyoteh, grabs his breastplate, and he and his friend drag the two Flint girls into the forest. I can hear the girls' screams for a long time.

Wrass is rocking back and forth, holding his bloody hand.

Chipmunk crawls over and says, "Wrass, let me look at it?"

Shaking, he pulls the finger from his wadded cape and extends it. It's still bleeding badly.

Tutelo's eyes go wide.

Chipmunk scrutinizes it and says, "It's a clean cut. We just need to keep the evil Spirits from infesting it. As we walk, I'll find a bear oak, shave one of the old knots, and brew you a tea. It will help."

Tutelo looks from Wrass, to the guards, and back to me, and sobs, "Odion? Let's run away! Hurry. Let's run!"

I glance around at the warriors, and my throat closes up. I lean close to her ear to whisper. "Soon. But not now. *Not now!*"

18

Just before dawn Koracoo rolled over, shook Gonda's shoulder, and whispered, "It's time. Let's rise."

Exhausted, shivering with cold, Gonda heaved a sigh and sat up. The frost-coated clearing glittered with the first blue rays of dawn. Beneath the oak trees, ten paces away, the sleeping body of Sindak made a dark hump. The sight surprised Gonda. Sindak must have moved out into the trees in the middle of the night, but Gonda hadn't heard a thing. Towa stood a short distance from where Sindak slept, watching the trail.

As Gonda stumbled to his feet, he whispered, "Will you wake Sindak, or should I?"

"Let's get the fire built and heat up the leftover cornmeal gruel from last night. I suspect with all of our clattering, he will wake himself. Or Towa will wake him."

Gonda reached down, picked up his weapons' belt, and tied it around his waist. It was colder this morning, and he thought he caught the fragrance of snow on the breeze. Dark Cloud People sailed the heavens.

He walked to the fire pit and grabbed a stick from the branch pile they'd collected last night. "The first thing this morning, we should clarify their duties with our new allies."

"I thought you did that last night."

Sheepishly, he said, "Did you hear that?"

"Most of it. You sounded like an idiot."

Gonda glanced over at Sindak. "I was defending your honor, my former wife. And I wasn't the only idiot there. Sindak is impulsive. He's the one most likely to act on instinct without thinking first. He reminds me of me at his age."

Koracoo pushed short black hair behind her ears. "I know that."

"Well, I was young." Gonda used his stick to stir the ashes from last night's fire. It took twenty heartbeats to separate out the warm coals and pile them in the center of the pit. As he began laying twigs over the coals, he softly said, "Did you get any sleep?"

She knelt across the fire pit from him. Her face looked haggard, her dark eyes dull. "Not much.

Towa and I stared at each other for most of the night. He's hurt and afraid."

The sound of their voices woke Sindak. He sat up and stretched, then turned to look at Towa. Towa had worn his deer-hide sling while he stood watch to keep his wounded arm from shifting. Towa whispered something to Sindak, who yawned and nodded.

Koracoo's eyes narrowed.

"What's wrong?"

"While I was staring at Towa last night, I had time to think about them."

"About Sindak? Or Towa?" He bent over and blew on the coals until the twigs caught and flames burst to life. He added more twigs, then lifted the tripod with the boiling bag and moved it closer.

"About Sindak, Towa, and Atotarho," she replied. "I still don't know why he chose these two. They are not physically suited to the task. Because of his injuries, Towa is not a reliable fighter. And they are friends—probably best friends. That means that when Towa gets in trouble—and that will be moments into the fight—Sindak will forget his responsibilities and concentrate on protecting his friend."

"Leaving you and me to rescue the children." Gonda added a branch to the fire and watched the flames leap around the new tinder. Sparks flitted into the deep blue predawn sky. "If you're right, what are we going to do about it?"

"Plan ahead, prepare for when it happens."

"Then you'd better threaten them thoroughly to start with."

"I plan to."

Gonda pulled two sticks from the woodpile and reached into the boiling bag to remove the cobble, which he placed at the edge of the flames to heat.

Then he turned to watch the two young warriors. Towa winced as he removed his sling, picked up his quiver, and slung it over his shoulder. Sindak was speaking softly to him while he adjusted his weapons' belt. Towa's braid hung down the back of his elk-hide cape. Though he had a handsome face, Gonda decided it was slightly feminine. His eyelashes were too long and his chin too pointed. Sindak, on the other hand, kept his right hand propped on the hilt of his belted war club. That told Gonda a good deal about him.

Gonda added two more branches to the fire—enough wood that the flames crackled. When he looked back at Koracoo, he could see the thoughts roiling behind her eyes. They had known each other long enough that they often entertained the same thoughts, and he suspected he knew what was bothering her. "So. What conclusions did you arrive at? How much of Atotarho's story did you decide you believe?"

"Very little."

He frowned at the fire. "I arrived at the same conclusion. That complicates our plan."

"In more ways than one." She used her chin to indicate Sindak and Towa. "How much do you think they know?"

"About Atotarho's plans? Probably nothing. But we need to find out."

"Yes. Just in case this turns into a brawl, we should loose our clubs."

"Don't you think that's a little obvious? They'll think we plan to crush their skulls."

"Depending upon what they do or do not know, we may."

"Now you're talking like a Standing Stone war chief." Gonda untied his club and rested it within reach near the tripod. He started to stand up.

"No, stay seated."

But Koracoo stood, untied CorpseEye from her belt, and propped it on her shoulder.

Towa and Sindak noticed, started murmuring to each other, and loosed their own clubs.

"Are you ready?" Koracoo quietly asked.

"Of course."

19

Sindak gripped his club and whispered, "I don't like this. They look too eager to see us."

"They probably just want to say good morning."

"I don't think those are happy expressions on their faces—they're murderous."

"You're imagining things. They just started breakfast. Nobody wants to fight on an empty stomach."

A soft morning breeze whispered through the trees, shaking the branches and swirling brown oak leaves across the clearing. Sindak studied Gonda and Koracoo. They had their capes hooked back over their weapons' belts, which made it much easier to swing their clubs. Sindak's eyes lingered on Koracoo. With her red cape pulled back, he could see her brown war shirt beneath... and the curve of her hip and the outline of one long muscular leg. Looking at her affected him like a Spirit plant in his veins. His pulse pounded, and his mouth went dry. The only thing that ruined the image was CorpseEye resting on her shoulder.

To Towa he whispered, "Why do you think they loosed their war clubs?"

"Maybe they heard something in the forest?"

"Maybe they heard us. That would certainly explain why Gonda looks like he swallowed a handful of rabbit droppings."

"Well, don't worry about it. We'll find out soon enough. In the meantime, let's pretend there's nothing wrong."

Sindak casually lifted his warclub and rested it on his shoulder, mimicking Koracoo's position. "I'm not good at pretenses, Towa."

"Just make the effort, will you?"

"Right up until someone jumps me."

Towa brazenly walked toward the Standing Stone warriors, wading through knee-deep leaves. The colors stirred up by his feet were stunning: brilliant scarlet, pale yellow, and a red so deep and dark it looked purple. As well as a hundred shades of brown. When Gonda saw Towa coming, he stood up...and Koracoo walked a short distance away to stand beneath an oak tree.

"I don't like it," Sindak whispered to himself, and stalked after Towa with his eyes narrowed.

As they entered the clearing by the fire, Towa said, "A pleasant morning to you," and circled around to stand opposite Gonda.

"And to you," Gonda replied. The firelight flickered from his clenched jaw and heavy brow.

Sindak glanced to where Koracoo stood, then gave Gonda a solid appraisal. Their positioning reminded him of a war council, where one warrior was always stationed a few paces from the fire so he could leap forward and smash somebody in the back of the head if necessary.

Towa smiled uneasily, knelt, and rested his club across his lap; then he extended his hands to the flames to warm them. "It's frigid this morning."

"Yes, and I fear I smell snow on the wind," Gonda replied. He almost sounded friendly.

Sindak continued to stand, glancing from Gonda to Koracoo. Gonda appeared tense, but Koracoo's face might have been cut from stone. She wore no expression at all.

Sindak and Gonda stared at each other in uncomfortable silence for a time; then Gonda gestured to the fire and said, "Please, sit down, Sindak. Warm yourself."

Sindak waited for Gonda to slowly drop to a crouch before he did the same. He glanced at Gonda's club, which rested near the tripod, within easy reach, and clutched his own more tightly in his hand.

"We didn't have time to talk about the children's trail last night," Towa said. "Is it close?"

Gonda pointed to the northwestern edge of the clearing. "Right over there."

Towa twisted around to look. "Does it head east or west?"

"Due east."

Sindak gazed at Koracoo again. She hadn't moved a muscle. It was unnatural. And he swore CorpseEye was watching him. The red cobblehead had two black spots that resembled shining eyes. "Well, we should eat and be on our way."

"Yes, as soon as possible." Gonda reached into his belt pouch, pulled out his wooden cup and a buffalo horn spoon, and set them aside. Then he pulled a stick from the woodpile and proceeded to stir the half-frozen bag of gruel. Ice crystals shished.

Towa and Sindak glanced at each other, drew their cups from their belt pouches, and waited.

After an agonizing amount of silence, Towa smiled and asked, "Why is Koracoo staring at us like that? She looks like a hunting cougar."

Despite her chopped-off hair, she was tall, beautiful, and dangerous. Threat seemed to ooze from her.

Sindak replied, "Yes, Gonda. She looks like

she's trying to decide whether or not to pounce on us and rip out our throats."

"What makes you think that?" Gonda said.

"I've seen that look before. I was married to Puksu."

Koracoo stepped forward, met each man's gaze, and said, "While the cobble heats up, let's talk about our goals."

Towa blinked. "I assumed we were going to track the children, find them, and rescue them."

"That's the ultimate goal, yes. But we're going to take it one day at a time. No running ahead. No guessing. I want only facts. We've had a lot of strong winds, as well as rain and snow. In many places, the trail will have vanished. Each of us must pay excruciating attention to the ground, or we'll never find the trail again."

Towa gave her a disgruntled look. "We know that. You don't have to explain to us as though we are five-summers-old boys."

Sindak said, "What Towa means, War Chief, is that we are warriors. So let me assure you that I am an expert tracker, and Towa is a genius with strategy."

Under his breath, Gonda said, "And modest, too."

Sindak smiled at him, but it was a promise of death.

Koracoo continued, "Good, Sindak. This is the

plan, then: I will lead and Gonda will bring up the rear. You will walk along paralleling the south side of the trail, and Towa, you will walk on the north side. Today, we stay close together, no more than fifty paces apart. If one person finds an interesting track, call out. The rest of us will work our way over to you. Do you understand?"

Towa squinted. "Of course we understand."

Sindak asked, "But...are you sure that's a good idea?"

Koracoo's brows lifted, and the forest seemed to go silent. "I take it that you don't?"

"I mean no disrespect, War Chief. I am just worried that they may suspect they are being followed."

Koracoo shifted CorpseEye to her other shoulder, and Sindak's fist instinctively tightened around his war club.

Koracoo said, "If the children were ordinary slaves, their captors would be herding them to villages to be adopted into new families. The warriors would be moving fast, interested only in getting home as quickly as possible. They wouldn't be paying any attention to their back trail. On the other hand—"

"If their captor is Gannajero, it's prudent to assume the worst," Sindak finished the sentence for her. "Which means she's watching her back trail like a hawk."

Koracoo nodded. "Yes. She can afford no risks. She has been pursued before, many times. She must expect it as a matter of course."

"So she may have scouts watching us even now?" Sindak asked.

"It's possible."

Towa exhaled hard, and his long braid sawed up and down his back. "Then is it wise for us to stay bunched so closely together? If we fan out, they may get one or two of us, but it will be hard to kill us all."

"I want you within my sight at all times. A lone warrior is far more vulnerable, Towa. If we stay together, we can defend each other. So, for now, we stay together."

Gonda reached over with two sticks, pulled the cobble from the fire, and dropped it into the gruel. Steam gushed up, and the bag boiled furiously for several moments before it settled down.

The delicious aroma of jerky filled the air. Sindak enjoyed it for a moment before asking, "That means, of course, that when she's sure we're following her, she'll attack us."

Koracoo's hard eyes sent a tingle up his spine. "Expect an ambush, Sindak. If we're on Gannajero's trail, it will be there. Maybe not today or tomorrow, but eventually she will take measures to eliminate us. Believe it. Prepare for it."

Sindak held her gaze. There was a strange,

hypnotic light in her eyes. He wouldn't mind seeing that every day of his life.

Koracoo added, "Just obey my orders, and I promise you that you will live through this."

"We have sworn to obey you, War Chief, and we will," Towa said. "Do you doubt that?"

"No, Towa. I'm just practical. It is one thing to swear it before your chief, but quite another to actually obey an enemy war chief in the midst of battle. But I hope you do..." She lowered CorpseEye to her side and took a new grip on the shaft. "Because you will be the first people I kill if you don't."

Wind swept through the forest and blew smoke into Sindak's eyes. He turned his head away for a moment, and it gave him time to consider her threat. Koracoo was right to worry that in the heat of battle, he might choose to do what he thought best, regardless of her orders. Because he might. These were Standing Stone People. His enemies. He'd been taught that from birth. Not even his chief's orders could overcome a lifetime of hatred and distrust.

Koracoo seemed to read the tracks of his souls. She walked around the fire and crouched less than three hands from Sindak. He could smell her faint fragrance, a mixture of wood smoke and something spicy, as though she'd washed her cape in water scented with spruce needles. She carefully propped CorpseEye across her lap and said, "Is that true, Sindak? Do you know your duty?"

"I know my duty, War Chief." He smiled.

She smiled back, but it didn't reach her eyes. "Good. Now that we understand each other, let's eat and talk about other things. Please fill your cups."

Gonda filled his cup, then backed away from the boiling bag. Towa came forward next, filled his cup, and went back to kneel in his former position.

Sindak tied his club to his weapons' belt and cautiously rose with his eyes still on Koracoo. Her gaze followed him, unblinking, like a lynx watching prey. He went to the bag to fill his cup, then said, "May I fill yours, War Chief?" He extended a hand.

Koracoo slipped her cup from her belt pouch, rose, and walked around the fire to give it to him. He filled it. When he handed it back, their fingers overlapped. Conflicting emotions danced across her beautiful face: suspicion, desperation, determination. They stood side by side, the contact lasting much longer than he'd intended. By the time she tugged her cup from his clenched hand, blood rushed in his ears.

Koracoo turned away. "Eat as much as you can hold. It's going to be a long day."

Sindak exhaled the breath he'd unwittingly been holding and walked back to crouch beside

Towa. He ate without a word, while Towa blew into his cup and studied Koracoo from the corner of his eye. Her cheeks had flushed. Towa gave Sindak an uncomfortable look.

And Gonda was glaring pure death at him. Who would have guessed that a man's face could contort like that?

Sindak drank his gruel with one hand on his war club.

Somewhere out in the trees, a hawk shrieked, and the call carried in the stillness.

Koracoo tilted her head to listen, and Sindak had the feeling that she suspected it might not be a hawk, but a warrior's signal. The hawk called again from the same place, and Koracoo relaxed and knelt near Gonda. She propped CorpseEye over her knees and sipped from her cup. Sindak continued listening for a time longer.

After a few more bites, Koracoo said, "Towa, as the chief's representative, I'm hoping you can help me understand some things."

Towa lowered his cup. "What things?"

"Your chief's recent Trading mission seemed foolhardy."

Towa straightened. "Why?"

"Warfare is rampant throughout our country. Why would your chief take his young daughter with him?"

Towa shrugged. "He loves her. I think he just

wanted her close. He often took Zateri with him on trips."

While she chewed a bite of jerky, Koracoo looked away from them, methodically surveying the oaks. "I find that strange. But then, I don't believe in coincidence."

"What do you mean?"

"I mean it makes no sense that a chief would risk the life of his daughter for a few bags of pearls and salted seafood. You live in rich lake country. A wise man would have stayed home, eaten lake trout, and worn freshwater pearls until the trails were safer. There must be another reason he undertook the Trade mission."

Sindak could see the hot blood rushing to Towa's face, and he understood it. She was either calling their chief a fool or a liar.

In a surprisingly calm voice, Towa answered, "We have more mouths to feed than you do, War Chief. Our people are hungry. Our harvests were poor this autumn. Any village with food is holding onto it with a granite fist. Atotarho knew that the only way he might be able to acquire more food was if he went himself."

"And he took sixty warriors to make sure the party was safe. Sixty of our *best* warriors," Sindak added.

Gonda looked up. "Best? I thought you two were there?"

Sindak had the overwhelming urge to tear his heart out.

Koracoo swung CorpseEye suggestively, which kept Sindak from carrying out his urge.

She continued, "Atotarho could have hired the finest Traders in the land. He didn't have to go himself."

Dawn's gleam had started to shade the forest, blushing color into the black branches and the autumn leaves that blanketed the ground. As the air warmed, the scents of wet bark and moldering leaf mat grew stronger.

Finally, Towa said, "Perhaps it would help if you understood some things about Chief Atotarho."

Koracoo nodded. "Anything you can tell me will be helpful."

"He was once a great warrior, but about ten summers ago, his joints began to stiffen."

"That's why standing is so difficult for him? I thought it might have been a battle injury."

"No. Evil Spirits have crept into his joints. When he could no longer serve as a warrior, he became a Trader, and he was very good at it. He loved Trading. I suspect he didn't think anyone could do a better job. That's why he didn't hire Traders. Ever."

Koracoo continued to eat at a leisurely pace, filling her horn spoon, putting it in her mouth, chewing. She appeared to be totally absorbed by her own thoughts.

Gonda, on the other hand, was watching them over the rim of his cup, and his eyes had an alert glitter.

Sindak angrily drank the last of his breakfast, and then he grabbed up a handful of leaves, wiped out his cup, and stuffed it back in his belt pouch. Koracoo's questions had him thinking, which he hated. He always got into trouble when he tried to think something out. But...there was something amiss here. Even if Atotarho loved to Trade, he did know how dangerous the trails were. Undertaking the expedition was very perilous. First of all, it left the village with sixty fewer warriors, which meant it was more vulnerable to attack. Second, Atotarho could have waited for another moon to undertake the journey. They had enough food for a moon, and raiding always died down in the winter, though the snow also grew deeper. What had been so important about the Trading mission that he felt obliged to risk his daughter's life, and the lives of sixty warriors, and the safety of their village?

Towa set his half-finished cup of soup on the ground, as though no longer hungry, and laced his fingers over one knee. After several moments of hesitation, he said, "Let me see if I understand you, War Chief. Are you suggesting that Atotarho wanted his daughter to be captured?"

"That's the only thing that makes sense to me, Towa."

"He loved her. Why would he do that?"

Koracoo drank the last dregs from her cup, then turned it upside down on the frosty grass to drain and replied, "I don't know."

"When you spoke with him, did he seem genuinely concerned about his daughter?"

"He did. In fact, he seemed terrified for her safety."

"Then her capture must have been an accident."

Koracoo didn't respond.

Gonda asked, "Where was War Chief Nesi when the girl was taken?"

Towa looked at Sindak. When Sindak shrugged and shook his head, Towa replied, "We were under heavy attack. We were trying to stay alive. I don't know where he was."

"Under heavy attack?" Gonda unlaced his belt pouch and tucked his cup inside. As he tugged the laces tight again, he frowned. "Who were they? How many warriors did they have?"

"I'm not sure." Towa glanced at Sindak again, silently asking if he knew.

Sindak said, "Maybe eighty. Maybe one hundred. Some of them were Mountain People, I think. The rest, I don't know. I didn't recognize the designs they wore. Why?"

Gonda's mouth pursed with disdain. He stood, lifted the boiling bag from the tripod, and walked around the fire to empty the final drops into Towa's cup. "Who was assigned to protect the chief's family?"

"Nesi and a hand-selected group of warriors." He picked up his cup again and took another sip.

Gonda said, "How many hand-selected warriors were in Nesi's group?"

"Five, I think."

"You *think?*" Gonda's brows plunged down over his flat nose. "You're a warrior. You should know."

"Well, I don't," Towa snapped.

Gonda stared down at him through slitted eyes. "Was the chief at the head of the expedition? Or was he walking in the middle, perhaps at the rear?"

"In the middle where he was surrounded by warriors."

"And where were you and Sindak?"

"We were last in line."

"So you didn't really see much of what happened around the chief's family?"

"Well...no."

Gonda rolled up the boiling bag and tucked it into his pack. "Did the attack come from the rear?"

"The bulk of the warriors struck the center and stole the chief's daughter, but at least thirty warriors attacked the rear. Both attacks happened simultaneously."

Koracoo gracefully rose to her feet, and Gonda stood up beside her. Instinctively, Sindak gripped his club.

In a low voice, probably meant for Gonda's ears alone, Koracoo said, "It *was* well organized. That's why they were chosen." Then she turned and headed across the clearing toward the place Gonda had indicated earlier, the place where they'd seen the children's tracks.

Gonda started to follow her, but Towa lunged to his feet and caught Gonda's arm as he passed. Gonda stopped, and eye-to-eye, they stared hard at each other.

"What did she mean?" Towa asked.

Gonda glanced at Koracoo, apparently to make sure she couldn't overhear them, then softly replied, "You're here because you were too far away to have played a role in the kidnapping. You are also young fools. You actually believe Atotarho sent you along with us to help rescue his daughter."

"Why else would he have sent us?"

Gonda pulled loose from Towa's grip. "I want you to think long and hard about that."

He walked away, leaving Sindak and Towa standing by the fire.

Sindak propped his hands on his hips and

glowered after Gonda. "You should have slit his throat. He's an arrogant fool."

Towa reached up to massage his wounded shoulder. It must have hurt, because he squeezed his eyes closed. In a pained voice, he said, "Gonda is not a fool."

"Of course he is. The chief sent us to help rescue his daughter. Nothing more."

Towa adjusted the strap of his quiver and expelled a breath. "Sindak, how many warriors in Atotarho Village are better, more experienced fighters than we are?"

"What difference does it make? The chief chose us."

"Yes, but why?"

He gestured lamely. "He trusts us."

Towa murmured, "I don't think so. I think Chief Atotarho fears there's a traitor in his midst—a very powerful man who has the loyalty of many warriors. But you and I are not among them."

Sindak shifted his weight to his other foot. "What are you talking about?"

Towa bowed his head and sighed as though surprised it had taken him so long to figure it out. "I'm talking about two young fools who are not part of that 'inner circle.' Young fools who still believe what their chief tells them."

"But if Atotarho doesn't trust us, why would he

give you his sacred gorget? He wouldn't risk losing that!"

Towa placed his hand over the gorget and looked down. "I don't understand that part yet."

"Even if you and I are the only two warriors Atotarho doesn't suspect of treachery, the gorget is too precious to risk on fools. He *must* trust us."

Towa murmured, "It's possible. But I doubt it," and walked toward where Koracoo and Gonda knelt, scooping leaves from the trail and piling them to the side.

Sindak stood rigidly for a few moments. If there was a traitor, a man who commanded the loyalty of many warriors, the logical choice was Nesi. But Sindak did not believe Nesi capable of such treachery. He'd fought at Nesi's side for five summers and seen only an honorable, if touchy, man striving to protect his people. Why would Nesi betray his chief?

"If not Nesi, then who?" Sindak asked, heaved a frustrated breath, and walked toward Towa.

20
ODION

In the dream, I wake to the sound of Father's hushed voice...

"I'm going," he says. "Who will watch your back? There's no one else—"

"I need you here, Gonda," Mother answers softly. "I want you to be in charge of defending Yellowtail Village."

I sleepily blink at the firelight reflecting from the bark walls of the longhouse. Almost everyone else is asleep. Someone close by is snoring softly, and I hear my little cousin, Ganahan, mewling as Aun Tawi fusses to get her to nurse. Grandmother Jigonsaseh is muttering softly in her dreams. I smile. These are pleasant sounds, the sounds of early morning in the Bear Clan longhouse.

I yawn and roll to my back. Forty hands above me, tied to the roof poles, ears of corn, whole bean plants, pawpaws, squash, and net bags of puffballs and mushrooms hang. They were picked a moon ago and already have the black coating of soot that protects them from mold and insects. Through the smoke holes, I see a few of the campfires of the dead glittering.

When I inhale a deep breath of the smoky air, I smell corn pudding, and my heart sinks. This is the dish Mother makes for us when she's going away on a war walk. It's my favorite. Made from parched corn mixed with chunks of maple sugar and roasted pumpkin, then boiled in hickory nut milk, it is a special sweet breakfast.

I turn my head to look at Mother and Father. They sit by the fire with their backs to me. While Father stirs the pudding with a wooden spoon, Mother quietly places food in her belt pouch: a bag of venison jerky, another of dried blueberries, two cornmeal biscuits, and several dried lichens wrapped in bark. I heave a sigh of relief. She's only going to be gone for the day —just a scouting mission close to the village. If she were going to be gone for longer, she'd be filling her pouch and her warrior's pack. Her quiver of arrows and bow rest atop her red cape at her side. Corpse-Eye, her war club, lies diagonally across them.

Father whispers, "Who are you planning to dispatch as scouts?"

"Coter and Hagnon. They're careful."

Father expels a breath. "Please, reconsider? If we

keep all six hundred of our warriors in the village, we can repel any attack that comes. Perhaps we should—"

"We have to know for certain, Gonda. It's the end of harvest. Our people need to be in the fields gathering the last crops from the dead plants, not huddling behind the palisade in fear."

"I know, but—"

"Gonda, if the trader was right, and he really did see Mountain People warriors skulking around our village, they were probably scouts assessing our harvest. If they discover that we had an excellent harvest, they'll be back to take it. We need to capture them and find out who sent them. There could be a war party out there just waiting for those scouts to report back. I don't want to give them the chance."

Father hesitates for a long time. He stirs the pudding, then in a low, disgusted voice, says, "It's probably Yenda, that two-footed piece of filth."

Mother's long black braid saws up and down her back as she nods. "That is my guess, as well. His People are very hungry, and he's a cunning war chief."

"Cunning?" Father scoffs. "He's a cowardly weasel. He's bent on destroying us, and every other member of the Standing Stone nation. The Mountain People would starve us to death if they could. We should kill every one of them."

Mother's mouth tightens into a hard line. "You don't mean that."

"Oh, yes, I do. I want all of the Mountain People dead, as well as all of the Flint, Landing, and Hills Peoples."

Mother's voice is barely audible as she replies, "You've become a warmonger, Gonda."

"Yes, and I wish you were, too. Once all of our enemies are dead, we can live peaceful lives."

Mother draws up a knee and laces her fingers around it. She is very tall for a woman, and I've heard many of her warriors say she's beautiful, "in a frightening sort of way." She has an oval face, with full lips and large black eyes. She doesn't say anything, though Father seems to be waiting for her response.

Father irritably tosses another branch on the fire. The wood crackles and spits as the sap burns. He is a medium-sized, slender man with a round face and long black hair. The folds of his plain buckskin cape catch the firelight.

Mother softly says, "The Hills People just attacked White Dog Village. Soon we'll be flooded with starving refugees. Half of our harvest will be gone in less than a moon. Don't you want this to end, Gonda? The warfare must end. Soon. Or we will all be dead."

Father lightly shakes his head. "Instead of worrying about feeding refugees, you should be worried that we're Chief Atotarho's next target."

Atotarho is an evil sorcerer from the People of the

Hills. A cannibal who adorns himself with human bones. He scares me.

Slowly, the images forming in my head begin to take on a horrifying reality. Atotarho could attack tomorrow. Even tonight. This is my greatest fear. I often have nightmares of our village being attacked, Mother and Father killed, and Tutelo and me being marched away as prisoners. Panic rises and overwhelms my heart. It begins to slam against my ribs. *Father is right! We have to kill them first. Before they can attack us!*

"Gonda," Mother says, "try to imagine what it would be like if all of our Peoples were united. If one village had a good harvest and another didn't, we could pool our food, and share it. No child would ever have to be truly hungry again. Not only that, we would be the greatest power in the land. No one could defeat us."

"Don't be ridiculous. We're too different to get along."

"There can be brotherhood in diversity. Brothers can respect each other's differences, even honor them."

Father lets out a low, disdainful laugh. "You're a dreamer, Koracoo. We'd never be able to cooperate long enough to discover each other's differences, let alone—"

"We must try, Gonda. It's our only hope."

Father looks unconvinced. He scowls at the fire. "I

will tell you one thing for certain, my wife. I will *never* take food from my own children's mouths to give to my enemy—not even if our elders order me to do it. I want the Hills, Flint, Landing, and especially the Mountain People to starve. And so does everyone else in this village."

Sadness lines Mother's face. She bows her head. Her gaze is faraway, as though she is seeing a peaceful world where everyone has enough to eat, and she knows it can never be. "It's people like you who make our future precarious, Gonda."

He snaps, "And people like you who make *today* precarious. Forget about the future! Start thinking about who we have to kill to keep our People alive for another moon!"

Mother pulls the laces on her belt pouch tight, then slips it around her waist and ties it. "I'm going to take three hundred warriors. We'll be home by dusk. I'll leave you the other three hundred. That should be enough warriors to allow you to hold off any attack Yenda can muster."

Father doesn't answer.

Mother says, "Keep every warrior inside the palisade until I return. Do you understand?"

Father turns to glare at her. "What makes you think I would disobey one of your orders? Have I ever disobeyed you?"

"No, but your tone of voice tells me that this morning you'd like to, just to spite me."

Father opens his mouth to say something hostile, and I rise up in my hides and croak, "Mother? I—I'm scared. Are we going to be attacked?"

Father's mouth purses. He gives me a glance that makes me long to run away and hide. He says I'm always scared, and that I'll never be of any use as a warrior.

Mother comes over, sits down, and gathers me into her arms. After she kisses my forehead, she says, "Don't be scared, Odion. Here, let's play a game. I want you to try and imagine a world where all of our Peoples are united and there is peace. Can you imagine such a world?"

I lean against her and close my eyes, trying hard. On the fabric of my souls I see people moving about villages, smiling. Dogs and children running happily across plazas. "I want to," I answer. "I don't like being afraid." I cast a glance at Father, who is shaking his head.

Mother strokes my black hair gently. "Someday there will be peace. I promise."

A profound sense of relief washes through me, as if something has opened in my chest and all the fear has drained away. I believe her.

Perhaps her way is better? All of the agony, the indecision, and the premonitions of disaster fade— vanishing amid the wave of peaceful firelight that now seems to fill the longhouse. The bark walls glitter as sparks float upward toward the smoke holes in the roof. People's faces shine, and now I hear laughter and loving voices as people begin to wake.

All I want is to stay here forever in the warm circle of Mother's arms, dreaming about a time when all the Peoples will be one, and no one will ever be truly hungry again.

"How do we make peace, Mother?" I whisper so that Father doesn't hear, and look up into her dark eyes.

Mother smiles down at me and whispers back, "We hold our tongues and listen. We open our eyes to the tears of others. We act out of stillness, not out of anger or—"

In a low hiss, Father says, "War Chief Koracoo, the blessed *Peacemaker.*"

There is such loathing in the word that I freeze as though I've suddenly seen a snake.

Mother lifts her head to look at Father. They glower at each other.

I want to run away again. Instead, I bury my face in the folds of leather over Mother's shoulder and just breathe. If I dream hard enough, I'm sure my soul will find a way to walk to that peaceful world Mother longs for.

When I close my eyes I can almost...

Mother pats my back and says, "I love you, Odion. I'll be home for supper."

I swallow hard. "Be careful, Mother."

"I will." She kisses my cheek, releases me, and rises to her feet.

As she goes over and slips on her red cape, Father says, "If I'm engaged in the middle of a pitched battle when you return, perhaps you should just trot up to Yenda and tell him you want to make peace? I'm sure he'll be happy to sit right down and negotiate like a good boy."

Mother slings her bow and quiver over her left shoulder, picks up CorpseEye, and walks from the longhouse without a word.

When she's gone, Father drops his head into his hands and quietly curses himself: *"When did I turn into such a fool?"*

As I pull up my deer hide and stare at him over the silken rim of tan hair, I wonder if he is a fool. Or if he's right that Mother is the fool for believing that peace is possible between the Peoples who live south of Skanodario Lake.

Father stirs the pudding again, and I let my gaze drift around the longhouse. Along the walls, melon baskets make dark splotches. Before the frost, we dig up melon vines with unripe fruit, and replant them in baskets of sand. During the winter, the melons ripen. They are Healing plants. We keep them for the sick.

Father calls, "Are you still awake, Odion?"

"Yes, Father."

He pulls a half-full ladle of pudding from the pot and blows on it. "Why don't you come over and taste this for me? I think it needs more maple sugar. What do you think?"

I smile, throw off my hides, and run to taste the pudding. Father puts his arm around me and hugs me as he brings the ladle to my lips...

Somewhere in the depths of my souls, I hear warriors moving around a camp, and realize I am dreaming, remembering the morning of the attack on Yellowtail Village.

I struggle not to wake.

21

Two days later, Sindak knew for certain they had lost the trail. He floundered around, weaving back and forth through the falling snow, searching for the slightest hint that even one man had passed this way—let alone an entire war party herding a group of unwieldy children. Blessed Spirits, how had Gannajero managed to conceal the trail? They had followed a wide swath of tracks until mid-morning; then a dozen trails had split off from the main one. They'd gone in every direction, as though men were abandoning the party, heading home to different villages. Gonda had argued vehemently for following one particular trail, and though Sindak had disagreed, Koracoo had ordered that they go with Gonda's choice. Gradually it had narrowed to the width of one man's path, and soon after, vanished.

Sindak was not the only one frustrated and discouraged. Koracoo knelt at every snapped twig, picked it up and examined it, then gently placed it back exactly as she'd found it. In the rear, Gonda was down on his hands and knees, crawling with his nose practically touching the snow that filled in the trail; and to Sindak's right, Towa stood beside a snow-rimed mountain laurel, studying it for broken branches, or the smallest fibers left from clothing.

When Towa glanced across the trail and found Sindak staring at him, his brows lifted. Sindak shook his head in answer to the unspoken question: *Have you found anything?*

Towa moved on to a thicket of dogwood.

White veils spun through the chestnuts and basswoods that lined the trail. Already the snow was over Sindak's ankles, and growing deeper by the heartbeat.

Though he knew it was futile, Sindak started wading through the drifts again, searching. He spotted a few hickory nuts and tucked them in his belt pouch.

"I found something!" Gonda shouted. As he brushed at the trail, he called, "Koracoo? Come quickly."

She worked her way back to him, carefully stepping in her own tracks so as not to disturb anything that might be hidden on the trail beneath the snow.

Sindak and Towa also walked toward him.

They all arrived at about the same time and stood in a triangle, looking down at Gonda. His forehead was furrowed, and deep lines engraved the corners of his brown eyes. He had his finger placed below a badly washed-out track.

Koracoo knelt and began brushing away the surrounding snow.

They all crouched and brushed at the thick coating of snow and leaves near the "track." As he scooped away the snow, Sindak grimaced. Hundreds of might-be tracks dotted the frozen soil, but there was nothing that he would even remotely assess as being made by a man. He turned to stare at Towa. Towa shrugged and rose to his feet.

Koracoo spent a long time scrutinizing the indentation Gonda had found. All the while, Gonda watched her with desperation in his eyes, obviously praying that she would say it had been made by a child.

Koracoo expelled a breath, shook her head lightly, and got to her feet. "This is nothing, Gonda. We've lost the trail. We all know it."

"But it's the best track we've found," Gonda objected. "We should break off branches and start sweeping every step of the ground."

Sindak waited. Surely Koracoo knew Gonda's

suggestion was folly. They were all exhausted and hungry. It would be far better to make camp and start fresh in the morning after a good night's sleep.

Koracoo looked up at the flakes swirling through the air. "We have perhaps a half-hand of light left. Let's stop for the day."

"What!" Gonda exploded. "We can't stop! We have to keep looking! The snow is growing deeper. By morning, their trail will be completely hidden!"

Koracoo's gaze wandered over the forest and came to rest upon a big pine. The area beneath the thick branches was dry and clear of snow. It was the best place to take shelter for the night.

Gonda seemed to sense her decision. "Koracoo, no. Please, let's keep searching." He gave her an imploring look, begging her to listen to him, to keep going.

Somewhere out in the forest, a turkey gobbled. Koracoo turned toward the sound, and Sindak hoped she'd order him to hunt it for supper.

Instead, she said, "No, Gonda. Let's make camp and fill our bellies with what's left in our packs. We'll start again at dawn tomorrow."

"But, Koracoo, we can still—"

"No, Gonda."

"You're being hasty! Think this through before you—"

"Sindak?" She turned to him. "Could you and Towa start cracking dead branches from the trees and piling them in the dry area beneath that big pine?"

"Yes, War Chief."

Sindak and Towa trotted away from the trail. As they snapped off the lower dead branches from two elm trees, they piled them in the crooks of their left arms and watched the interplay of emotions on Koracoo's and Gonda's faces.

"You're wrong," Gonda said through gritted teeth. Every muscle in his thin, wiry body had contracted and bulged through his cape and leggings. "We should keep searching as long as we have light. Every moment we rest or delay, our children—"

"That's enough, Gonda," she said, trying to keep her voice low. "Come. Let's go over and clean out some of the pine duff for a fire pit."

As she started for the pine, Gonda called, "You blame me, don't you?"

She stopped and turned to face him. "For what?"

"At that last fork in the trail, Sindak wanted to go left, but I insisted we go right. You would have taken the left fork, wouldn't you?"

Koracoo stared at him, her face still and desolate.

Sindak whispered, "Dear gods, the panic in his voice gives me a stomachache."

Towa's shaggy brows drew together. He whispered back, "If it does that to you, imagine how Koracoo feels. But he's right—your trail was the better choice. If he hadn't argued so vehemently..."

Koracoo softly said, "Gonda, I was the one who made the final decision to take the right fork. Not you. If it was the wrong choice, I am to blame. But we will not know that until tomorrow when we go back over our tracks and find the place where we erred."

Gonda shook his fists as though he longed to scream at her to ease his own fears. After four or five heartbeats, he replied, "You don't trust me, do you?"

Exasperated, she threw up her hands, then turned and walked to the pine, where she ducked beneath the overhanging branches and crawled back into the dry shadows.

Gonda trudged through the snow and crawled in behind her. "Koracoo, answer me."

She propped CorpseEye against the trunk, then unslung her pack and quiver, laid them aside, and used both hands to start digging a hole for the fire pit in the pine duff. Even in the dim light, the red cobble-head of CorpseEye gleamed like old blood.

When she just kept digging, Gonda reached out, and his hand tightened around Koracoo's wrist like shrunken rawhide. "I know what you're thinking. Just say it."

Sindak and Towa both went rigid.

Koracoo lifted her gaze to Gonda. Death lived in those dark eyes.

Gonda released her as though he'd been holding a poisonous serpent, then slumped to the ground, breathing hard. "Forgive me. I didn't mean to—"

"You're arrogant, Gonda." Koracoo resumed digging. "It has always been your failing. One of these days, it will cost you—or someone you love— his life."

"You mean *their* lives, don't you? Our children?"

She crawled away and began breaking off the dead branches at the base of the trunk, tossing them into a pile near the fire pit.

Gonda watched her expectantly, then dropped his face into his hands. "If you hadn't left, our village would have been able to withstand the attack. This is all your fault, Koracoo."

Her eyes filled with such a deep, aching sadness that Sindak had the insane urge to run over and wrap his arms around her. The fact that she'd kill him stopped him.

He placed another branch on the big bundle in his left arm. "I can't hold another twig, but I'll feel like I'm interrupting a private argument if I go back now."

Towa stepped up beside him with an even

larger bundle cradled in his arms. "Don't worry. Our arrival will be a relief to both of them. Let's go."

They trudged down the hill and ducked beneath the pine boughs. As they worked their way back to the scooped-out hollow, neither Koracoo nor Gonda watched them. Sindak and Towa dumped their armloads by the pit, and Sindak looked askance at Gonda. He hadn't moved. He sat with his hands over his face.

"I'll start the fire," Towa said. "Sindak, can you gather some needles and twigs for tinder?"

"Of course."

Sindak went around collecting handfuls of old pine needles and twigs, which he piled beside Towa's right moccasin.

Towa unslung his quiver and set it near Koracoo's; then he arranged the tinder in the pit and removed two fire-sticks from his pack. He placed the punky stick on the ground, took the pointed hardwood stick and set it in its notch—a prepared hole in the punky stick—and began spinning the hardwood between his palms. The air was damp; it took around five hundred heartbeats for the friction to create an orange glow in the punky wood. Towa kept spinning the hardwood stick until the glow expanded and began to crackle; then he dumped it onto the nest of twigs and dry needles and softly blew on them until flames curled up.

Sindak knelt near the woodpile and extended his hands to the faint warmth. From the corner of his eye, he watched Koracoo. All night long he'd had erotic fantasies about her. It was hard to shove them out of his mind as he watched her remove the boiling bag from her pack and tie the long laces to the tripod. Every move she made had a distinctive, muscular grace that brought back his dreams with aching clarity. When she finished, she carried the tripod over to the fire and set it up near the blaze. "How much food do you have left in your packs?"

Sindak said, "I have a little dried fish left."

"And I have some venison strips."

"Good. I have some hard cornmeal biscuits, baked with blueberries and sunflower seeds. Let's throw in everything we have, heat the soup, and fill our empty bellies so we can sleep warm."

"Yes, War Chief. Did anyone see a good rock for the bag?"

"I did." Towa rose, ducked beneath the overarching limbs, and went out into the trail to kick loose two small rounded rocks.

"Gonda?" Koracoo said. "What's left in your pack?"

He lowered his hands and looked at her with hollow eyes. "A few bear cracklings."

"Please throw them into the boiling bag."

Gonda unslung his pack and dug around until he found the small hide sack that held his dried food. He upended the sack over the boiling bag and shook out every morsel that remained.

Towa carried the two rocks back, ducked beneath the sheltering branches of the pine, and rolled the rocks into the fire.

"We need water," Koracoo said. She untied the buffalo paunch canteen from her belt and emptied it into the boiling bag. As she pulled the canteen's laces tight again, she said, "You'll each need to add more water from your own water bags."

"I have some left." Sindak emptied his canteen into the bag. The rest would be frozen by morning anyway.

As Gonda tipped his canteen over the bag and water trickled out, he said, "Koracoo, we need to discuss—"

"Tomorrow, Gonda. I'm going to bed. Sindak, please take first watch."

"Yes, War Chief."

"You're not going to eat?" Gonda squinted at her.

"I'm more tired than hungry. I'll eat in the morning."

She crawled over to CorpseEye, gripped her club, and went to the opposite side of the tree trunk, where she rolled up in her cape and propped CorpseEye across her chest.

As darkness fell, snow gusted down the trail and the forest branches clattered together. Towa and Sindak watched the rocks at the edge of the fire, waiting for them to warm up.

"We'll all feel better after we eat," Sindak said. "Hand me your cups. I'll pack them with snow and set them near the flames to melt, then I'll add the water to the bag. Even if the soup is watery, there will be more for breakfast."

Gonda didn't move. He stared at the flames with haunted eyes. Towa handed Gonda's cup to Sindak. Sindak packed it full of snow and sat it near the rocks to warm. Gonda didn't seem to care. He kept twisting his hands in his lap.

What a difference. Last night, he was an offensive wolf. Tonight, after losing the trail, he's a trembling ruin of a man.

Sindak said, "Give me your cup, Towa."

22

Towa handed over his cup and went back to staring at Gonda. In the firelight, the muscles of Gonda's jaw quivered.

Sindak crouched down on the opposite side of the fire and filled his own cup. The limbs gave them just enough room to sit up straight. As the wind blew the branches, the radiant halo of firelight shifted, casting shadows across their faces and creating strange dark wraiths in the snow that gusted by.

Towa asked, "What did you do, Gonda?"

He lifted his head, and guilt lined his round face. "What do you mean?"

"Koracoo doesn't trust you. Why?"

Anger hardened Gonda's mouth. "That's none of your concern. I—"

"If she does not trust you, how can we? Do you

have a weakness we should know about? Forgive me for asking, but in the heat of battle, such knowledge may save my life."

Gonda seemed to be weighing what he should and should not say, and Sindak found that curious. Any other man accused of being weak would have reached for his war club and started swinging. Last night, Gonda would have. But not tonight. He turned away, dug his horn spoon from his pack, and twisted it in his hands. "I made a mistake."

"A mistake?"

"Yes."

"A mistake that led to the destruction of Yellowtail Village and the loss of your children?"

Gonda looked like he wanted to talk about it but didn't have the strength, or perhaps he couldn't figure out how.

Towa said, "I had children once, Gonda. A brave little boy and a sweet, beautiful girl. I lost them both, along with my wife, to a fever two summers ago. I have some idea what you must be feeling."

Gonda's expression softened, but he did not look up.

Sindak frowned at Towa. He never talked about the loss of his family. Ever. It hurt too much. What was he doing? Trying to create some kind of tie with Gonda?

Gonda swallowed hard and softly said, "Do you still live the nightmare of their deaths, Towa?"

"Every day."

As Gonda brought up one knee and propped his cup on top of it, he kept his gaze on Towa's somber face. "Then perhaps you can imagine what it would be like to live the nightmare of your children's lives as Gannajero's slaves. Every instant, I see my children hurt, or hungry, or being tormented by enemies. Or I fear they are dead, and their souls are out wandering alone in the forest, calling out to me, trying to find their way home."

Towa's breath misted in the air. "That must be like having a belly full of obsidian flakes."

The scent of the campfire grew stronger as the night deepened and smoke hung in the pine boughs just over their heads.

Sindak said, "They may have just been captured by an ordinary war party, and are being well cared for. No man mistreats a child he plans to adopt into his own family."

Gonda squeezed his eyes closed. "I pray you are right."

Towa gave him some time before he added, "And even if the children are with Gannajero, they're alive. They're too valuable to kill. We *will* find them and bring them home."

Towa picked up the rocks with two sticks and dropped them into the bag. Steam exploded. When the boil settled down, he dumped the melted snow from their cups into the bag and waited a few seconds, then dipped their cups full of soup and handed each around the fire.

Gonda's cup halted halfway to his mouth. "We may bring them home, Towa, but I'm not sure even our best Healers will be able to cure them."

Out in the forest, frozen trees cracked and snapped beneath the brunt of the icy wind, but Sindak pinned his attention on Gonda's agonized face. Brief, hard flurries of sleet had started to whip by just beyond the pine. Gonda seemed to be watching the veils of snow as they careened down the trail.

Sindak asked, "What was the mistake you made?"

Gonda set his cup down and rubbed his hands over his face. In a voice almost too low to hear, he said, "I disobeyed an order."

Sindak shifted, and the frosty pine needles at his feet crunched. "What order?"

When Gonda didn't answer, Towa said, "When we accompanied Atotarho on the trading expedition, we heard rumors that Mountain People war parties were scouting near Yellowtail Village. You must have heard them, too."

Through a long exhalation, Gonda said, "A Trader came through the morning of the attack and told us he'd seen Mountain warriors just a short distance from Yellowtail Village."

"What did you do?"

"The only thing we could. Koracoo took half our warriors out to verify the rumors. They could have been false. She wanted to make certain."

"But you did not go with her?"

Gonda stared absently at the ground. "No. I was in charge of defending the village."

A sleety gust rattled the branches over their heads. Sindak flipped up the hood of his buckskin cape and cradled his warm cup in both hands.

Towa softly asked, "What happened?"

Gonda cast a surreptitious glance at Koracoo, and Sindak had the vague feeling that Gonda hoped she might come to his rescue by answering that question herself. When she did not, he heaved a heavy sigh.

"She ordered me to keep all of my warriors inside the palisade until she returned."

Towa's brow furrowed. "You didn't?"

Gonda took another bite of soup and took his time swallowing it. "Just moments before the attack, two terrified scouts came running into the village, claiming there were over one thousand enemy warriors in the forest. I didn't believe it. There couldn't be that many."

"*One thousand?*"

He gritted his teeth. "It didn't take long

before... When the palisade was on fire in fifty places, and I could see them massing for a final assault, and I panicked. Their eyes glinted in the starlight. I led half my warriors outside to create a diversion, to try and lead them away—"

Sindak said. "That's ridiculous!"

Gonda hung his head. "At the time, it seemed like the right decision."

A cold shiver went down Sindak's spine. Among the People of the Hills, the penalty for disobeying your war chief's orders was death. If he had disobeyed Nesi's orders and half the village had been slaughtered as a result, Nesi would have paraded Sindak from longhouse to longhouse and allowed those who had lost family members to take out their vengeance on Sindak's flesh. The torture would have lasted for days.

On the other hand, a desperate man facing overwhelming odds had no choice but to believe in his Spirit Helpers. Obviously, Gonda's had let him down.

Towa said, "What happened to the warriors you led outside? Were they killed?"

Gonda tightened his grip around his cup to still the tremors in his hands. Barely audible, he answered, "A few of us survived."

Against the firelit background of whirling sleet, Gonda appeared miserable and haunted. His round face was worn down to its heavy bones. He couldn't have seen more than twenty-six or twenty-seven summers, but in the short black hair that covered his ears, scattered filaments of silver caught the light.

Sindak said, "Afterward, there weren't enough warriors inside the palisade to defend the village, were there?"

He shook his head. "It was overrun with stunning swiftness."

Even now, days later, he must still see the tormented faces of his dead friends and relatives. Or was he thinking of his children? Perhaps hearing their last cries?

Sindak said, "So, Koracoo blames you?"

"I'm sure she believes that if I'd kept all of our warriors inside the palisade, as she ordered, I might have been able to hold out long enough for her war party to get back and turn the tide of battle." Gonda turned his cup in his hands.

"She's wrong, Gonda."

"You can't know that. You don't know her."

A faint roar underlay the keening wind. They all tipped their heads to listen to it. It resonated like the thrumming bass note that seems to linger in the air long after the song is finished, more felt in the bones than heard.

Towa said, "Gonda, my people believe a war chief should be a good enough judge of character to know when a man isn't suited for great responsibility. Nesi would have never put you in that position."

Sindak shifted slightly to look at Koracoo. He wondered if Towa had not inadvertently hit upon the problem: *Koracoo can't forgive herself for leaving Gonda in charge. Perhaps it isn't Gonda she distrusts. She's lost confidence in herself.*

Gonda hung his head and shook it. "I was perfectly suited. I've done it dozens of times. Koracoo made the right choice in selecting me for the duty. I just...I—I..."

Towa kept glancing down to where Gonda's hands gripped his cup as though to strangle the life from it. "I don't know you very well, Gonda, but among my people, you have a reputation for valor and brilliance in war. In fact, none of our warriors wishes to face you in battle."

Gonda stared at Towa with his jaw clenched.

Towa seemed to be worried about how to phrase it. "Men make mistakes in the heat of battle. Koracoo knows this better than anyone. So, my question is, why doesn't she believe it was a mistake? Earlier, she called you 'arrogant.' Does she think you disobeyed her orders to spite her?"

Gonda's nostrils quivered. He rose unsteadily to his feet, wiped out his cup, and said, "Ask her. Maybe she'll tell you." He tramped away.

Sindak watched him roll up in his cape and prop his head on his pack. Just before he closed his eyes, he grabbed his war club and dragged it close.

A powerful gust of wind blasted the forest, and a branch broke in the fire. The scattering sparks threaded Towa's handsome face with crimson light. Sindak studied his taut expression.

Quietly, so Gonda could not hear, Sindak said, "I'm surprised he told you as much as he did."

"I'm not. Gonda's been desperate to discuss this with someone. The guilt is eating him alive."

Sindak considered that. His grandmother had once told him to make carelessness his enemy and righteousness his armor, because guilt was like a dull blade twisting in the gut; it would kill, but it took a long time and the pain was unbearable.

Towa added, "I can't wait to hear Koracoo's side of the story."

Sindak gave him an askance look. "Never, my friend."

"No? Why not?"

Sindak's brows lowered. Barely audible, he answered, "Because if there were one thousand enemy warriors outside Yellowtail Village, her returning forces would have been ambushed and destroyed long before they could reinforce Gonda. From the moment she left, her village was doomed."

"Do you think she knows that?"

"Maybe."

In the shadows on the other side of the tree trunk, he could just make out Koracoo's face. It had a pale gleam. Short locks of black hair fell over her cheeks. He thought her eyes might be open. Was she watching them? Trying to hear their discussion?

Towa set his empty cup beside the fire pit, rose, and walked over to stretch out near Gonda.

Sindak's gaze returned to Koracoo. He swore she was watching him. Firelight reflected in her open eyes. He just couldn't be certain if she was looking at him, or out into the forest. His gaze drifted to the trees, where wind-thrashed limbs created such a noise an entire war party could be upon them before they heard a whisper of moccasins on the leaf mat. Stealthily, his right hand lowered to the war club tucked into his belt.

Koracoo closed her eyes.

The dull blade twisting in her guts must be excruciating.

Sindak finished his soup and crawled to the edge of the pine boughs to keep watch on the trails.

23

Sometime around midnight, a groan woke Koracoo. She rolled to her side and looked at Gonda. He'd been making soft agonized sounds for over a hand of time—probably fighting the battle again, trying to save the village over and over.

Her gaze shifted to Sindak. He was no longer sitting beneath the pine where the flames could blind him to the night, but had moved to stand outside, facing east, looking up the trail. The sleet had stopped, leaving the deep blue sky clear. As the icy breeze gusted through the trees, Sindak's buckskin cape billowed around his broad shoulders. Though he clutched his war club, he also carried his slung bow and quiver.

Gonda made a sound like a suppressed scream.

Sindak glanced back over his shoulder, shook his head, and went back to watching the trails.

Koracoo stared out past Sindak to the stars visible just over the tree-tops. They glittered as though silver flames burned in their hearts. *Where are you, Mother? Are you alive or dead?*

Her mother's half-dead eyes seemed to be branded on her souls— always there, always pleading for help. She'd found her injured Mother lying in the charred remains of their longhouse with Koracoo's sister, Tawi, beside her. For the rest of Koracoo's life she would wonder whether or not Tawi had been trying to pull their mother to safety when the burning wall had collapsed on top of them.

Koracoo released CorpseEye where it rested across her chest and put her hands on either side of her head, pressing hard, endeavoring to force some sense into her worry-laced soul. She felt like a sleepwalker, just going through the motions of life, not really here.

"Come on," she hissed. "Wake up. Wake up!"

By now, the Yellowtail Village survivors would have arrived at Bur Oak Village, and rumors would be running wild. They'd blame her for the attack. They'd say that if she'd left Deputy Deru in charge, instead of assigning Gonda, their families would be alive—which was probably true. They'd say she'd depended upon the wrong man, that she'd favored him because he was her husband, and it had cost them everything...Or they'd say she should have never left on the scouting mission the morning of the attack.

She looked at Sindak, Towa, and Gonda. When the fight came, could she depend upon any of them? The only person she was absolutely certain she could depend upon was herself, which meant she would have to be the linchpin of any plan. What would happen if she fell? Which of them would take over and rescue the children?

For thirteen summers, she had known the answer to that question. The fact that she no longer did terrified her. Memories were her greatest enemy. One, from three summers ago, kept replaying over and over. It always started the same way. She saw the forest fire reflected in Gonda's eyes. The rest of their war party had been killed during the first day of fighting. She and Gonda had been running through the burning trees for four days, trying to find a safe way home—but Flint warriors had cornered them in a narrow rocky canyon. When Koracoo had fled there, she hadn't noticed that it dead-ended twenty paces back. They'd scrambled behind a tumbled pile of boulders, and the victory cries of the Flint warriors had been deafening...

"How many are out there?" Gonda had asked as he'd checked the arrows in his quiver. Sweat matted his black hair to his round face, making his nose seem longer.

"I'd guess fifteen or twenty."

"I hate to tell you this, but that's fourteen more than I have arrows for."

"And fifteen more than I have." She'd pulled CorpseEye from her belt.

As the warriors clambered through the rocks around them, Gonda had given her a grin. "I've heard the elders talking. You're going to be war chief someday soon. Surely the future war chief of Yellowtail Village can figure a way out of this trap."

Koracoo had laughed. He'd always done that to her—made her laugh in the most dire of circumstances. Five arrows simultaneously battered the rocks around them, showering them with rock chips. They'd both hit the ground and covered their heads.

When she'd dared to look up, she said, "Absolutely. Are you ready?"

He'd given her a surprised look. "What are you going to do?"

"I'm going to climb over these rocks and start bashing out the brains of any warrior who leaps up to face me."

"That doesn't sound like a very sound strategy to me. There are a lot of arrows flying out there."

"Would you rather wait here?"

He'd rolled to his hands and knees. "No, I

wouldn't. But before we die, I want you to know that you are everything to me. If we die here—"

"Stop being sentimental. Tell me tomorrow." She'd jumped up and started swinging CorpseEye.

He'd been right behind her...

Koracoo forced the memory away, but not before an incapacitating ache filled her chest.

As though he knew, Gonda whimpered.

Koracoo listened, her heart pounding. He was not a coward, nor stupid. But by disobeying her, he had broken her heart and betrayed her trust. She vacillated between longing to beat him to death with her bare fists, and bury her face against his chest and weep until she had no tears left.

For days, she'd secretly endured the same fear that lived in his eyes—the fear that they would never find their children, or that Odion, Tutelo, and Wrass were injured, or being tortured. Worst of all was the knowledge that their children were lying awake at night, praying that she and Gonda were on their trail coming to save them.

Even worse, *even worse*, every time Gonda looked at her, his eyes were reverent with faith in her. He believed Koracoo would save their children.

As the knot in her belly tightened, she quietly rose and went to stand beside Sindak. He kept his gaze on the trail. She guessed his age at eighteen or nineteen summers. His shoulder-length black hair gleamed in the starlight, and his lean face reminded her of an eagle's, beaked, with sharp brown eyes.

Without looking at her, he said, "My watch is not over. You have another hand of time to sleep, War Chief."

Koracoo studied the faint crystalline haze that filled the air. Amid the swaying branches, elusive winks of stars flashed. "At dawn, we will go back and take the left fork in the trail."

"Very well."

By the glow of the fire, she could see every small line of his face, from temple to jaw, thrown suddenly into shadow. It made him look older, and more sure of himself. He turned, and curiosity glinted in his brown eyes.

"What is it, Sindak?"

"I was just wondering, that's all."

"Wondering about what?"

He used his chin to gesture to Gonda. "Why did you bring him on this journey? It's hard on him. And will be harder still if we don't find the children."

"He'll survive."

"Will he? I suspect you can stand whatever life throws at you, Koracoo. I'm not sure he can. Every step we take, I feel like I'm watching him fall apart. One day he's desperate to fight me, the next he barely has the strength to keep hold of his club."

Koracoo's fingers unconsciously moved over

CorpseEye, caressing the fine dark wood like a lover's skin. Sindak glanced down, noticed, then apprehensively lifted his gaze to her eyes again.

She said, "This journey may be hard on him, Sindak, but it is also his redemption."

"Even if we fail?"

"Especially if we fail. At least Gonda will know that he did everything he could to save them."

"Not if he is the reason we don't."

She propped the cobble-head of CorpseEye on the ground and leaned against the shaft like a walking stick. Power tingled beneath her fingers. When it grew too uncomfortable, she shifted her grip. It might just be the warmth of the wood against her freezing hands. Then again, CorpseEye could be trying to get her attention, to tell her something. She scanned the trees. The forest appeared calm, and she heard nothing unusual.

Sindak said, "What's wrong?"

"Nothing...it's just...nothing."

He glanced up the trail. "Your expression suddenly changed, War Chief. You looked worried. Why?"

Koracoo petted CorpseEye. Sindak watched with an intensity she found unsettling. "CorpseEye is old," she said. "He often hears or sees things I do not. When he does, he tries to get my attention."

"How?"

She gestured uncertainly. "Power flows from CorpseEye into my hands. It's a warmth. At times, it's painful."

"Was it painful just now?"

"Don't worry about it, Sindak. I'll search after you've gone to sleep. I'll have lots of time before dawn. That way if it's nothing, I—"

Sindak walked out onto the trail, where the starlight gilded the arrows in his quiver-like points of flame. His cape flapped around his long legs. "Let's search now."

Koracoo followed him.

The gusting wind had blown the snow and sleet into drifts and exposed patches of the forest floor. Dark, irregular blotches of soil marked the trail.

She said, "It will be far easier to search at dawn."

"You said we would head back to the fork in the trail at dawn."

"We will, unless we find something here." She swung the club up to rest on her right shoulder. "Truly, Sindak, you should get some rest."

"I won't be able to sleep until we know it's nothing."

"All right, we'll head east."

Sindak nodded.

Starlight coated the ground and reflected from the snow with blinding strength. Koracoo concentrated on the places that had been blown clean. They hadn't been able to see those patches earlier in the day.

As she searched, her thoughts strayed to Gannajero. She'd been thinking a lot about her as they'd tried to work out her trail. The mysterious old Trader had survived for forty summers, which meant she was shrewd. She probably kept eight or ten men around her, but no more. A few wary, trained warriors were necessary. They could move fast, and shoot enough arrows to allow Gannajero to escape. More than ten were just loose ends that would need to be disposed of later.

Including herself, Koracoo had four warriors, and only one was fully functional. A draining emotional haze clouded her vision, as well as Gonda's, and Towa had a wounded arm. It took every bit of concentration she had to try to think clearly. At the same time, she had to keep Gonda focused so that he didn't run off on some misguided mission of his own.

That was the other reason she'd brought him. He wouldn't have stayed home. No matter what orders she'd given him, he would have disregarded them and gone searching for their children.

Koracoo walked around a fallen log and saw, behind it, a smooth grassy meadow dotted with boulders. On the far side of the meadow, the mountainside sloped steeply upward. Several trees were down, probably blown over in last moon's storms. Their roots, ripped from the earth, stuck up like dark, crooked arms reaching for the heavens.

Koracoo's breath, her heart, and time itself seemed to stop. As if he'd heard something, Sindak looked over at her, then out into the darkness. For a long while only the hissing of her breathing filled the silence.

Then at the meadow's edge, near the blown-down trees, something glimmered.

She cautiously walked toward it. Sindak seemed to understand. He shifted his course to intersect her path.

"What did you see?" he asked.

"I'm not sure yet. A flicker, like a shiny string of polished blue beads, had caught the light just right."

As they approached, walking side by side, that twinkle came again, brighter this time, as though a stream of pale blue fire had raced down the length of the object.

Sindak murmured, "I see it."

Koracoo put a hand on his wrist, stilling him. "Let's go carefully now. It could just be a vein of quartz crystals unearthed by the falling trees, but it could be a decoration on a warrior's cape."

As they edged toward the twinkle, Koracoo saw a moose. It skirted the edge of the meadow in the distance, its eyes flashing as it trotted off.

"Stop!" Sindak hissed suddenly and thrust out an arm to block her way. His gaze had fixed on the snow two paces in front of them. "Do you see it?"

"What?" She searched the snow...and saw an unnatural shadow, running straight as an arrow's flight to connect with the pale blue line that sparkled at the base of the downed trees.

"It's a trail," Sindak said. "A deep trail. Despite the snow, you can still see the swale left by the passage of many feet."

Koracoo tried to fight down the hope that rose sweet and hot in her breast. "Let's make certain."

She went to stand alongside the swale. It was wider than it looked—ten hands across. Starlight glimmered from the frozen edges of the trail like white paint. "Whoever made this path is walking out in the open, going through meadows and probably across bare rock, loosely paralleling the trails."

"That's why we're having such a hard time staying with them. Should I wake the others?"

"No. Let them sleep." She propped her left fist on her hip. "We don't know that this is the children's trail. It could have been made by any stealthy war party."

"But you think it's their trail," he said.

"Yes," Koracoo said. "But we won't know until we can really examine the tracks. Come on. Let's go back. I'll start my watch, and you can rest. At first light, we'll pick up right here."

They walked back to camp, listening to their feet crunching the snow.

When they reached the pine, Sindak stopped and extended his hand to touch CorpseEye, but his fingers halted a hairbreadth away. "Is this all right?"

"You may touch him." Koracoo extended the club.

Sindak touched the cobble head, then gently ran his fingers over the carvings in the wooden shaft. An expression of wonder came over his young face. Could he feel the warm heart that inhabited the club?

Sindak said, "We'd have never found the trail without CorpseEye. At dawn, we'd have headed back to the fork in the trail, and gone the wrong direction."

She smiled faintly. *"If* this is the trail."

Sindak removed his hand and clenched it, as though to hold onto the sensation; then he looked at her.

Something about the softness of his expression touched her...and worried her. She'd seen that look before in the eyes of young warriors. Usually it was youths who had seen fifteen or sixteen summers. Sindak was a little old for this, but he knew her less well. At this point, it was just attraction, but if his gaze began to get that worshipful glow, she would have to do something about it. And afterward, he would never look kindly at her again.

"Get some sleep, warrior," she ordered.

"Yes, War Chief."

Sindak ducked low and crawled beneath the pine into the firelight. He pulled his rabbit-fur blanket from his pack and stretched out beside Towa. Towa said something too low to hear.

Their conversation woke Gonda. He grumbled, threw them hateful looks, then flopped to his opposite side and went back to sleep.

Koracoo spread her feet, heaved a sigh, and watched the trail.

24
ODION

Gannajero's shrill voice makes me sit bolt-upright. Crystalline snowflakes fall from a lavender sky.

Last night was freezing. I barely slept. All night long I lay with my body curled around Tutelo's trying to keep her warm while I listened to the terrifying sounds of the camp. Muffled sobs and cries filled the darkness.

I lift my head. I don't see any of Gannajero's warriors. By now, I have memorized some of their names: Kotin, Hanu, Galan, Tenshu, Waswan, Ojib, Chimon…But several of the gamblers remain rolled in their blankets, snoring. A few wander about unsteadily. Weapons clatter as belts are strapped on and quivers slung over shoulders. I watch two men walk into the forest. A short time later, the scent of urine carries on the wind. Where is Gannajero?

"Are you awake?" Wrass says softly.

I roll over. Snow coats the hood of his cape, encircling his narrow, beaked face with a white frame. A bandage wraps his little finger. "Yes, I'm awake."

He doesn't look at me. He points and I see Gannajero out in the trees. She's hissing at Hehaka and one of the Flint girls. Shaking her fist in their faces. The girl weeps.

"What's happening?"

"They're being punished."

"Why?"

"Hehaka was up all night. He was so tired he stumbled and sloshed corn brew on one of the warriors. I don't know what the girl did."

I sit up. Gannajero's warriors have gathered over a small fire. They already have their packs on, as though ready to march. "Are we leaving?"

"Yes, soon, I think."

"Where are we going? Did you hear them say?"

Wrass shakes his head. "No."

Several of Gannajero's men disperse into the trees. Each walks away alone, heading in a different direction. This makes me frown. While several gamblers are still sleeping, only four warriors remain. Two guard us, and two—Kotin and another man whose name I don't know—stand talking in the trees. "Where are they going?"

"They may be scouting the trail ahead."

"But they walked away in different directions."

"Maybe they're scouting the trails in every direction."

My heart pounds.

Gannajero grabs Hehaka and the Flint girl by the hands and drags them back toward us. She keeps growling at the girl. When she arrives, she shoves Hehaka to the ground and grips the girl's shoulders so hard the girl yips.

Tutelo jerks awake in terror and flings her arms around my waist. "Odion, what—"

"You little fool!" Gannajero shouts at the Flint girl. "If you ever try that again, I'll let the man kill you. Do you understand? If it weren't for me, you'd be dead right now."

The girl sinks to her knees and weeps. "Let me die. Please let me die?"

Gannajero kicks her in the chest, and the girl falls backward, making hideous choking sounds. She can't breathe.

For a few terrible instants, Gannajero's wild eyes fix on me. She leans forward and says, "After last night, you must be worried about your sister. Hmm?"

I can't find my voice. Terror has killed it.

Wrass says, "Where did the men take the other two Flint girls? Why aren't they back yet?"

Gannajero laughs and walks away.

The girl on the ground writhes, fighting for air.

Wrass crawls over to her. "Sit up. You'll be all right. She just knocked the wind out of you."

Tutelo looks up at me, and tangled black hair falls down her back. "What did that girl do, Odion?"

"I don't know."

Wrass helps the girl to sit up, and she finally manages to suck in air. As she breathes, her tears begin to subside. Except for the puffy red welt on her oval face, she's very pretty, with long eyelashes and a small nose. Long black hair sways around her.

"Are you all right?" Wrass asks.

"Sh-she sold my sisters. To the men who claimed them last night. They're gone!"

"She sold them forever? I thought she was just selling them for the night?"

"No. They're gone. I'll never see them again!"

"You don't know that. The men may take your sisters home and adopt them into their families," Wrass says gently. "And you are all right. That's all that matters right now. You—"

Tutelo says, "Why didn't she sell you?"

The Flint girl glances at Tutelo and chokes back a sob. "I—I found a rock on the ground and hit the man in the face. It left a gash. He tried to kill me."

Wrass says, "And Gannajero stopped him?"

"Yes. She said I was too v-valuable to die just yet."

From the far side of the group of children, Chipmunk rises on trembling legs. She walks over and squats in front of the Flint girl, then lifts a shaking hand to touch the swollen knot on the side of her face. "What's your name?"

"Baji."

"Where are you from?"

"S-Singleleaf Village."

Chipmunk gently strokes her hair. "I've studied Healing. I'll make a poultice from snapping alder bark. You won't even have a bruise. I promise."

I turn to watch Gannajero. She is packing up camp, collecting huge bags of trade goods—her payment from last night. When she finishes and piles all of her packs in one place, she stalks around camp, shouting curses and kicking sleeping men, forcing them to get up.

Hehaka draws my attention when he rolls to his side and seems to melt into the bed of leaves.

"Tutelo, I need to go speak to Hehaka. Will you be all right?"

She nods and releases me so that I can crawl over to Hehaka. "Are you all right, Hehaka? Are you hurt?"

He looks up at me with agonized eyes. His lean, starved face has gone pale. "She sucked out my soul," he whispers, and glances around, hoping none of the other children hear. But Wrass does. He turns to gaze at Hehaka. "She sucked it out with that eagle-bone sucking tube and blew it into the little pot that she carries in her pack."

"Why?" Wrass asks.

He squeezes his eyes closed. "She told me that when she kills me, my afterlife soul will never be able to find its way home. I'll be chased through the forests forever by enemy ghosts." Tears leak from the corners of his eyes.

"She's an old fool," I say in anger. "She's not powerful enough to do that. It would take a great shaman, and she's—"

"Shh!" He grabs my arm and shakes me hard. "You mustn't say that. She'll hear!"

"She can't hear me, Hehaka. She's way over on the other side of cam—" As I speak the words, Gannajero turns and stares right at me. Her eyes are like black suns burning me to cinders. My mouth goes dust dry.

"She's a witch!" Hehaka whispers. "She can hear voices from half a day's walk away. I swear she can. I've seen it."

Wrass moves over and crouches beside me, staring down at Hehaka. He holds his wounded hand protectively against his chest. "You've seen it? How long have you been her slave?"

"S-seven summers," Hehaka whispers.

Stunned, I hiss, *"Seven?"*

Wrass asks, "Why hasn't she sold you? Where do you come from?"

"I don't know." Hehaka shivers and covers his eyes with his arm so that he can cry unseen. "She won't let me go. I don't know why. She says she'll never sell me."

Wrass clenches his fists and whispers to me, "That doesn't make any sense. She's a Trader. That's what she does: sell children. Why would she keep Hehaka?"

I grip his arm and tilt my head, telling him I want to talk with him alone. Wrass rises. We walk a few paces away. The warriors guarding us straighten. One nocks an arrow in his bow. Another swings his war club suggestively.

I pull Wrass close to hiss, "Do you think she's a witch?"

Wrass swivels around to gaze at Gannajero. "She's evil, that's for sure. Do you think she really sucked out Hehaka's soul?"

I lick my chapped lips, taste blood, and glance again at our guards. They are watching us with half-lidded eyes. One wrong move and they'll kill us, just like they did Agres and her sister. "I don't know. Do you remember when old Pontoc lost his soul? Mother told me that his afterlife soul walked out into the forest and left his body like a moth flying away from a cocoon."

"But Pontoc couldn't talk after his soul left, and Hehaka is still talking."

We both turn to study Hehaka where he lies on the ground, shivering.

I say, "And Pontoc went insane. He started

sneaking up on people in the night and trying to strangle them."

We stare at each other. Wrass is probably remembering—as I am—the morning when Pontoc's own relatives dragged him screaming from the longhouse and clubbed him to death. They had to do it to protect their clan. The Standing Stone People followed the Law of Retribution. Murder placed an absolute obligation upon the kinsmen of the dead man to seek revenge by claiming the life of either the murderer or someone closely related to him. Since they traced descent through the female, the obligation fell particularly upon the murdered person's sisters, mother's brothers, and sisters' sons. If Pontoc had actually managed to kill someone, the victim's family would have had the right to claim the life of anyone else in Pontoc's clan that it wished to be rid of, including the chief or clan matron. No clan could risk that.

"We should keep watch on Hehaka," Wrass said. "If she really does have his soul captured in that pot, he'll go insane, and we'll need to protect ourselves."

"Yes, I think—"

My gaze lands on Chipmunk as she moves to kneel beside Hehaka. She speaks softly to him. Hehaka nods, as though whatever she said soothed him. As Chipmunk rises, she takes a deep breath, fixes her gaze on me, and walks forward. Her mourning hair clings to her round face in irregular locks.

Wrass sees her and frowns. "What's she doing?"

"Coming over here."

When she gets close, she bows her head so it's impossible to see her lips move, and whispers, "I can h-help. I know Healing plants."

"What do you mean you can help?" Wrass asks. "You mean you can help heal Hehaka and Baji?"

The girl nervously licks her lips. She's so scared she looks like she might faint. "No, I—I mean if you can get me close, I c-can..." She swallows hard, waiting for us to fill in the rest of the sentence.

In a stunning moment of understanding, I say, "Blessed gods, yes."

"What?" Wrass sounds annoyed.

I grab his arm and pull him very close to hiss, "*We can fight them.* With her help, we can escape!"

I turn to the girl. "What's your name?"

She swallows hard before she stutters, "Z-Zateri."

Wrass frowns at me and opens his mouth to say something unpleasant, but before he does, understanding widens his eyes. He stands perfectly still for a moment, staring at me. Then he glances between us, and in a dire voice, says, "If we do this, we'll only have one chance. We have to do it right."

A LOOK AT BOOK TWO:
SHADOWED FOREST

In their latest masterpiece, renowned authors W. Michael Gear and Kathleen O'Neal Gear delve into the chilling narrative of Native American protagonists facing an unfathomable evil.

Winter is settling over the autumn forests, but War Chief Koracoo and Deputy Gonda must not stop. They are facing a parent's worst nightmare: their children, Odion and Tutelo, have fallen into the hands of a legendary evil: Gannajero the Trader. Known as the Crow, she is a figure out of a nightmare, a witch who buys children from victorious warriors who've destroyed the children's villages and then she sells them to the highest bidders.

In Gannajero's camp, the kidnapped children have grown desperate. They are sure their families are coming to rescue them but it's taking too long. Can they find a way to save each other even if it means some of them must die so that a few may escape?

Dive into this riveting tale of bravery, sacrifice, and the enduring spirit of survival.

AVAILABLE MAY 2024

ABOUT W. MICHAEL GEAR

W. Michael Gear is a *New York Times, USA Today,* and international bestselling author of sixty novels. With close to eighteen million copies of his books in print worldwide, his work has been translated into twenty-nine languages.

Gear has been inducted into the Western Writers Hall of Fame and the Colorado Authors' Hall of Fame—as well as won the Owen Wister Award, the Golden Spur Award, and the International Book Award for both Science Fiction and Action Suspense Fiction. He is also the recipient of the Frank Waters Award for lifetime contributions to Western writing.

Gear's work, inspired by anthropology and archaeology, is multilayered and has been called compelling, insidiously realistic, and masterful. Currently, he lives in northwestern Wyoming with his award-winning wife and co-author, Kathleen O'Neal Gear, and a charming sheltie named, Jake.

ABOUT KATHLEEN O'NEAL GEAR

Kathleen O'Neal Gear is a *New York Times* bestselling author of fifty-seven books and a national award-winning archaeologist. The U.S. Department of the Interior has awarded her two Special Achievement awards for outstanding management of America's cultural resources.

In 2015 the United States Congress honored her with a Certificate of Special Congressional Recognition, and the California State Legislature passed Joint Member Resolution #117 saying, "The contributions of Kathleen O'Neal Gear to the fields of history, archaeology, and writing have been invaluable..."

In 2021 she received the Owen Wister Award for lifetime contributions to western literature, and in 2023 received the Frank Waters Award for "a body of work representing excellence in writing and storytelling that embodies the spirit of the American West."